CHINES

BY

ROBERT K. DOUGLAS

With Illustrations

GRAHAM BRASH, SINGAPORE

First published in 1893
This revised edition first published in 1990 by
Graham Brash (Pte) Ltd
227 Rangoon Road
Singapore 0821

ISBN 9971-49-165-6

Printed in Singapore by
Chong Moh Offset Printing Pte Ltd

CONTENTS.

INTRODUCTION.

(Revised, 1990)

CHINESE FICTION.

IT is impossible to say when the first story was published in China, but it is quite safe to assume that stories have been current from all time. There never was a land in which stories did not exist. Even the nomads of the deserts of Mongolia and of the still drearier wastes of Tibet attempt to vary the monotony of their existence by telling wierd tales as they crowd round their camp-fires. To such people the efforts of the imagination are to life what froth is to champagne. They keep it fresh and brisk, and impart liveliness to what, without them, would be flat and wearisome.

The earliest stories which we know of in China are those which are enshrined in the *Book of Odes*, the contents of which date back to the time of Solomon. In these ballads we find tales and fragments of tales which doubtless formed part of the stock-in-trade of professional story-tellers. Their themes are for the most part idyllic scenes of country life in which love, tempered with subdued passion, plays a prominent part.

To India the Chinese story-tellers owe much that gives lightness and variety to their works of fiction. Buddhistic fancies and the philosophical conceptions which underlie Brahmanism introduced new and interesting phases into Chinese literature. Indirectly, those supernatural and magical ideas which first made their appearance in the writings of Taoist sages, and which have since become a central feature in Chinese fiction, were derived from the same sources.

Chinese novels may be divided into two classes: historical and social. The most celebrated Chinese historical novel is the *San Kuo Chi*, or *History of the Three Kingdoms* by Lo Kuanchung of the Yuen dynasty (1268-1368). It is set in the period which covers the fall of the Han dynsaty (A.D.25-220) and the existence of the three states into which the empire was temporarily divided during the succeeding fifty-five years. This epoch was one of great disorder, with wars and rumours of wars on all sides. Probably no half-century in Chinese history has so bloody a record as that of this epoch. It is therefore a model period for the pen of a historical novelist, and Lo Kuanchung takes every advantage of the material at his disposal. With considerable skill he unfolds the complicated drama and moves the puppets, crowded on the stage, with precision and without confusion. The principal characters stand prominently forward, and the action of the plot goes on about them without the least obscuring their presence. Nor is the romance ever allowed to drop to the prosaic level of history. The more serious records of wars and political movements are lightened by a plentiful introduction of artistic by-play. By the exercise of the novelist's licence we are admitted into the palaces of the emperors, and are initiated into the secrets of court intrigues.

Even the imperial harems are thrown open for our benefit, and we are made confidants of the plots hatched in the busy brains of idle ladies, which on more than one occasion overthrew emperors and caused fire and sword to overspread the land. The supernatural also is largely included. Times of political disorder are generally favourable to superstition, and it is quite possible that Lo may have given only a picturesque colouring to the wonders and strange omens which were commonly reported at the time.

The social novel is of quite a different kind. The writers of romances of this order eschew battles and bloodshed. In their eyes, military prowess does not attract the applause of the people. A man is a model hero who takes the highest degree at the examinations, and quotes the classics with the greatest fluency. In addition, he must be clothed with virtue as with a garment, and cast behind him every temptation to evil, and however difficult may be the circumstances with which he is surrounded, he must invariably act in strict accordance with the "rules of propriety". He should venture all in the cause of oppressed virtue, and esteem it the highest honour to have exposed the wrong-doer. A typical novel of this kind is the *Hao Ch'iu Ch'uen*, whose hero is *Tieh*, or "Iron", and whose conduct is as inflexible as that metal.

In all Chinese novels there is plenty of movement in the plot, but the scenes are placed before the reader as a succession of tableaux; and though the action of the principal characters is sufficient to describe them in a general way, there is no close analysis of motive, and no gradations in their good and evil qualities. They are all either very black or very white. Half-tones are unknown, and the reader has to apply his knowledge of human nature to the events recorded.

One fault which is observable in all Chinese novels is the want of conciseness in the style in which they are written. Neither the readers nor the authors are in a hurry, and therefore the former are ready to accept and the latter to provide a prolixity and minuteness of detail which would be the ruin of any work of the kind published in the West. To a great extent the shorter tales of the Chinese are free from this defect. Authors who have to complete their plot within a given number of pages, have not the space to indulge in the prolix meanderings of their more elaborate brethren.

All Easterners are fond of stories. Whether in the bazaars of Egypt, under the village trees in India, in the temples of Burma or the market places of China, crowds are constantly to be found listening to the tales of wandering narrators whose reward varies in accordance with their power to amuse their audiences.

In China, where printing is cheap and the knowledge of letters general, of an evening when the day's work is done, a favourite amusement of the people is to listen to the tales from the *Liao Chai Chi I*, the *Chin Ku Ch'i Kwan*, or some other well-know collection, read by the better educated among them. The stories in the *Chin Ku Ch'i Kwan* are the best of their kind. In these, as in most Chinese stories, ghosts and magical appearances are favourite properties brought in with telling effect.

Unless a number of the stories are base misrepresentations, Chinese wives, down-trodden as they are in theory, manage to assert themselves in a most unmistakeable manner. (See "A Matrimonial Fraud".) Henpecked husbands are the most common butts of story-tellers, who never tire of representing the superior sex in most inferior positions. For example: A certain official underling one day drew upon himself the wrath of his wife, who scratched his face so severely that when he presented himself before his chief the next morning, the officer asked him the cause of his wounds. With ready wit the underling replied, "While taking my ease in my garden last evening a portion of the vine-trellis fell on me and scratched my face." The officer, who knew something of his domestic relations, at once divined the true cause. "Don't talk nonsense!" he replied. "It was your wife who scratched you." As it happened, his own wife had been listening to this interview behind the door and, in defence of her sex, burst in upon the scene. The officer, terrified by this invasion, said hurriedly to the underling, "Go away, never mind your wife; *my* vine-trellis is about to fall on me."

Female curiosity is another fruitful subject of these

anecdotes, and one is told in which this failing brought to a close a life almost as long as Noah's. According to Chinese tradition the king of Hades keeps a register of the lives of men. To each person is given a single page, and so soon as that is filled up, the person whose career it represents is at once called to appear before the dread sovereign. It chanced, however, that on one occasion the king, observing that the binding of his book required mending, tore out a leaf from the volume with which to repair the back. Chang, the man to whose career this leaf was appropriated, was thus overlooked and, the page not being filled up, he went on living until he reached the age of nine hundred and sixty two, when he had occasion to mourn the death of his seventy-second wife. This lady, being of an inquisitive turn of mind, had often been puzzled by the length of her husband's career and, on appearing in her turn before the king of Hades, she made bold to ask him for an explanation of such unusual longevity. The king at once ordered an investigation to be made, and the mistake being discovered, he filled up the page at once, and Chang's matrimonal ventures were incontinently cut short.

It is curious to find in many stories incidents which bear striking resemblances to events narrated in the Bible. The story of Balaam's ass is with variations reproduced in a well-known collection of Chinese tales, as is an incident bearing a likeness to the judgement of Solomon.

Farces are very popular with the Chinese people, who are possessed of a keen sense of humour and delight in the presentation of situations which provoke laughter. Theirs is generally not a subtle humour, stimulated by innuendo; they prefer the obviously funny.

Many of the foregoing remarks are aptly illustrated in the stories which will be found in the following pages. These stories have not been translated literally from the original. The plots and incidents have been faithfully retained, but the tales have been pruned and adapted. As illustrating the popular literature of China they have more than a passing interest. They hold up, as it were, a mirror to the life of the people, and thus bring home to our consciousness the fact that human passions and feelings are much the same on the banks of the Yang-tsze-kiang as on the shores of the Thames.

Robert K. Douglas
British Museum
1 November 1892

CHINESE STORIES.

A MATRIMONIAL FRAUD.

ADAPTED FROM A CHAPTER OF A CHINESE NOVEL.

ONE hot August afternoon the Prefect of Ping-chow might have been seen sitting in the verandah of his private apartments smoking his post-prandial pipe and admiring the flowers, which threw a fragrance and beauty over the courtyard which stretched before him. The official work of the morning had fatigued him. Litigants had been troublesome, and as witnesses had refused to give the evidence expected of them, he had been obliged to resort to the application of thumb-screws and ankle-squeezers. Having a natural repugnance to torture, its use always disturbed him; and after such occasions as the present, he exchanged his seat in the judgment-hall for his easy-chair and pipe with a redoubled sense of enjoyment. On this particular afternoon his wife, Mrs Le, was seated by him, and was recounting, among other events of the morning, the particulars of a visit she had received from a certain Mrs Wang.

"From the moment she entered the room I took a dislike to her," she said. "She had a fawning, catlike manner, with her 'May it please you, madam,' or 'May I be permitted to say, your Excellency;' and all the while that she was thus fawning on me and praising *your* learning and wisdom, I felt sure she had some object in coming besides the desire to pay her respects. Then she went on to say how rich her husband was, and how willing he would be at any time to advance you money in case you should need it. At last out came the canker-worm from this rosebud of flattery. Her son, it seems, is very anxious to marry a Miss Chang, the daughter of a rich President of the Board of War, who is at present engaged on service on the Annamese frontier. His suit is countenanced by the young lady's uncle, but is rejected by herself."

"And why?"

"Well, according to Mrs Wang,—but then I should not believe anything because she said it,—there is some clandestine love affair which disinclines her to the proposed match. As her father is away, it was necessary that she should be consulted, although, of course, her uncle would be justified, as Mrs Wang hinted, in arranging matters in his absence."

At this moment a servant entered the courtyard and presented to the Prefect a red visiting-card, on which was inscribed the name of Mr Wang, the father of the would-be bridegroom.

"Why, this is the husband of your visitor of this morning," said he, as he glanced at the card. "They are evidently determined to push on the affair. If they are as keen in the pursuit of virtue as they are of this marriage, they will soon out-virtue Confucius."

"My belief is," said his wife sententiously, "that they might dine off their virtue without breaking their fast."

"Well, at all events, I will go to hear what this man has to say; but having fortunately seen his hook, I shall refuse the bait, however skilfully he may throw the line."

The host and his guest were as unlike as it was possible for two men to be. The Prefect moved into the room with the manner of a polished gentleman,—one who, being well assured of his relative position, knew perfectly what was expected of him, and what he had a right to expect from others. He was tall too, and his refined features expressed a composure which was engendered by power and assured by habit. Wang, on the other hand, was his antipodes. He was short, stout, broad-featured, and altogether vulgar-looking. His eyes were small and ferret-like in their restlessness, while his natural awkwardness of manner was aggravated by a consciousness that he had come on a dishonest mission. As the two men met and bowed, the Prefect surveyed his guest with curiosity not unmixed with loathing, much as a young lady might regard a strange kind of toad. To his repeated requests that Wang would seat himself, that worthy feigned a constant refusal, until at last, in despair, the Prefect was fain to sit down, when his guest, with bated breath, followed his example. The progress of the interview was not more propitious

"The Prefect surveyed his guest with curiosity not unmixed with loathing."

than its opening. Wang attempted some classical allusions, but having but a vague knowledge of history, succeeded only in likening his host to the reprobate Chow-sin. Being a stupid man also, he was quite unaware of the contempt which was sufficiently obvious in the Prefect's manner, and he opened the real object of his visit with assurance.

"The presence of your Excellency in our district has shed a ray of golden light among us. But a lamp, as I well know, cannot give light unless it is supplied with oil. Now Mencius said—I think it was Mencius, was it not, your Excellency?—that out of their superfluity people ought to satisfy the wants of those not so bountifully provided for. If, then, your Excellency should at any time require that which it is within the power of your servant to supply, I beseech you to give him the gratification of knowing that he can be of service to you."

"As your classical knowledge is so profound," answered the Prefect, "you doubtless remember the passage in which an ancient sage declares that an official who receives anything, except in return for services performed, is a 'fellow.' Now it happens that I am not inclined to play the part of a 'fellow.'"

"Ha, ha, ha!" chuckled Wang, who thought this was a hint for him to state his business in full, "your Excellency I see, likes to come to the point. The fact is, then, that my son is deeply enamoured of a Miss Chang, whom he once saw from a window in her uncle's house as she walked in her garden. Her beauty has completely ravished him. He can neither eat nor sleep from the intensity of his passion, and his very life depends upon his marrying her. Besides, I don't mind saying to your Excellency that the connection,—her father is a President of the Board of War,—would be both agreeable and useful to me."

"I am sure I wish your son every success," said the Prefect; "but I cannot see how otherwise the affair concerns me in the least."

"Why, is not your Excellency the 'father and mother' of your people? and in the absence, therefore, of the President, it is on you that the duty falls of arranging a marriage for this young lady. As was said by Confucius, 'Every girl on arriving at a marriageable age should be betrothed;' and it is plain, therefore, that Miss Chang's bridal presents should be prepared. If your Excellency would deign to direct the betrothal of this young lady and my unworthy son, my joy would be endless, and my gratitude without bounds. I may mention, also, that Mr Chang, the young lady's uncle, who is in every way a most estimable man, cordially supports my son's suit."

"But why," asked the Prefect, "does the young lady decline the proposal which I understand you have already made her?"

"Well, the fact is," said Wang, "that she has formed a foolish attachment for a young man who some months ago met with a bad accident outside her door, and who was carried into her house to die, as every one thought. But, marvellous to say, by the doctor's care and the watchful attention of the lady's servants, he recovered. Unfortunately, however, his cure took some time; and during his convalescence, it seems that the two young people held several conversations together, always, I am bound to say, through an impenetrable screen, and in the presence of attendants; and she was so struck with his sentiments and appearance—for I am told that she managed to see him, though he never caught a glimpse of her—that she vowed a vow never to marry any one but him."

"And who was the young man?"

"His name was Tieh (iron); and he must have been as hard as iron not to have been killed by his fall, for he fell on his head and was kicked by his horse. He doubtless has a certain kind of ability, as he has just taken the third degree, or that of 'advanced scholar,' and was on his way home from his examination at Peking when he met with his accident."

"A certain amount of ability, indeed!" ejaculated the Prefect; "why, the whole capital rang with praises of his scholarship; and in his native town a tablet has already been raised, as a memorial of his conspicuous success. However, as you have appealed to me officially on behalf of your son, I will cause inquiries to be made, and will let you know my determination."

The Prefect was as good as his word, and the reports he received, both of the Wang family and of the young lady's uncle, were so eminently unsatisfactory, that he directed his secretary to write a short letter to Mr Wang, stating that he must decline to interfere in the matter.

On receipt of this note, the look of cunning which usually rested on the coarse and blurred features of the elder Wang, changed into one of furious hate. Never having been accustomed to exercise self-restraint in anything, his anger, like the many other passions which alternately possessed him, raged with unchecked fury, and he broke out with a volley of imprecations, calling down endless maledictions on the Prefect personally, and casting frightful imputations on the honour of his ancestors both male and female. Hearing his curses—for, like all Chinamen, Wang found shouting a relief to his feelings—Mrs Wang rushed in to know their cause.

"Nicely you managed matters with the Prefect's wife, you hideous deformity!" screamed her infuriated husband as she entered. "The hypocritical prig now refuses to have anything to do with the marriage, and has actually returned, without a word, the bill of exchange for a thousand taels which I enclosed him."

"And you don't seem to have done much better with the 'hypocritical prig' yourself," replied his wife; "but don't be a fool; cursing people's grandmothers won't do you any good, and certainly won't do them any harm. So just sit down and let us see what we had better do in the circumstances."

These words fell like a cold shower-bath on Wang. In his heart he was afraid of his wife, who was both cleverer and more unscrupulous than he was, and who, having been the instigator of most of his unrighteous deeds, was in possession of secrets which left his peace of mind, and even his liberty, very much in her power. In all such matters as were at present in dispute, therefore, she took the lead, and on this occasion sat herself down opposite her disturbed lord, and began—

"Well now, since we cannot expect any help from this pattern of assumed virtue, I think we had better try what the girl's uncle will be able to effect by cajolery. You must go to him at once, before the

"You hideous deformity!"

idea gets abroad that the Prefect is against us, and persuade him by promises of money to represent to his niece that he now stands in the place of a father to her, and that as such he strongly urges her to agree to the match.. Let him dangle every bait likely to catch our fish that he can think of. He should enlarge on our wealth, on our influence with the official classes, and on the good looks and engaging qualities of our son. Living so completely secluded as she does, she is not likely to have heard of his escapades, and Chang can at times lay the paint on thick, I know. But before you start, take a few pipes of opium to steady your nerves. Your hand shakes as though you had the ague, and you look like a man on the verge of the Yellow Springs."[1]

This last advice was so thoroughly congenial that Wang at once retired to follow it. His wife, having compassion on his quivering fingers, accompanied him to his study, and having arranged his pillow, proceeded to fill his pipe. With practised skill, she mixed the paste with a long needle, and gathering on the point a piece about the size of a pea, laid it neatly in the small orifice in the centre of the surface of the flat-topped wooden receptacle which protruded from the side of the long stem. When thus prepared, she handed the pipe to her recumbent husband, who eagerly clutched it, and applied the pellet of opium to the lamp which stood ready lighted on the divan. The effect of the first few whiffs was magical. His face, which a few moments before had been haggard with excitement, and twitching with nervous irritability, now softened down into a calm and placid expression; his eyes lost their restless, anxious look; and his limbs, which had been drawn up with muscular rigidity, relaxed their ten-

[1] *I.e.*, Hades.

sion. Once, twice, and thrice did Mrs Wang refill his pipe; and then, fearing lest a prolonged indulgence should disincline him to move, she urged him to rise and to pay his visit.

Refreshed and calmed, Wang arose. All his excitement had disappeared, and a sensation of pleasurable enjoyment, which threw a rose-tinted hue even on the present state of affairs, had succeeded to it. A very few minutes sufficed for the arrangement of his toilet. The application of a damp towel to his face and hands, a few passes of a wooden comb to smooth backwards the stray locks which had escaped from his queue, and a readjustment of his cap and robe, were all that were needed to fit him for his interview with Chang. As he was borne swiftly through the streets he leaned back in his sedan, lost in a reverie, in which he saw, as in a dream, his son married to the object of his admiration, himself decorated by the Emperor with a blue button in exchange for a few thousand taels; and the Prefect, bound hand and foot, being carried off to prison. Whether this last vision was suggested or not by an official procession which he encountered on the way, will never be known; for so lost was he in dreamy indifference to external objects, that he was quite unconscious of the presence of his arch-enemy in the same street, although his chair coolies had, as in duty bound, stood at the side of the road while "the great man" passed on his way.

Having been warned by a forerunner of the approaching arrival of Wang, Chang was waiting ready to receive him. Profoundly the two friends bowed to one another as they seated themselves on the divan; and after a remark or two on general topics, Wang went straight to the point. He related the Prefect's refusal to interfere, and then enlarged on the proposal indicated by his wife, and ended up by making Chang the offer of a round sum of money in case he succeeded in arranging matters with his niece. Chang listened patiently, feeling confident, from his knowledge of his guest, that a bribe would be offered him, and being well assured that it would be the inducement held out last, though in reality first, in importance. The sum named settled the question so far as Chang was concerned. He was a needy man, being considerably in debt; and besides, he foresaw that if he could once induce his niece to regard him *in loco parentis*, he would be able to get into his hands, for a time at least, the management of his brother's property. This trust, he knew well, might be turned to profitable account, and his eyes sparkled at the prospect that loomed large before him. When, therefore, Wang ceased to speak, he said, with effusion—

"I have listened to your commands, and have been overcome with admiration at the lucidity of your expressions, the knowledge you possess of the rites of antiquity, and the general wisdom of your views. It remains only for me to say that I will obey your orders to the best of my mean ability, and that I regard with infinite gratitude your munificent intentions towards your 'younger brother.' Let me now offer for your refreshment a pipe of 'foreign dirt.'"

Without waiting for assent Chang nodded to a servant, who, being evidently used to the habit, left the room and speedily returned bearing two small lacquer-trays, each of which contained an opium-pipe and the necessary adjuncts. By the side of both his master and Wang, who were now recumbent, he placed a tray, and then withdrew, leaving the two friends to the enjoyments of intoxication. Pipe after pipe they smoked, until at last their pipes dropped from their mouths, and they passed into the opium-smoker's paradise—a state of dreamy unconsciousness, in which strangely fanciful visions passed before their otherwise sightless eyes, and strains of sweetest music charmed and delighted their ears. It was late the next morning before they awoke, and it was then plain, from the expression of their faces, that the pleasurable sensations of the early part of the night had long since passed away. Their eyes, which were surrounded by broad black rims, bore a haggard and painful look. Their lips were blue and parched, and their complexions wore a mahogany hue, as though saturated with their favourite narcotic. Many "hairs of the dog that had bitten him" and some hours' quiet rest were necessary before Chang was in a fit condition to pay his visit of persuasion to his niece. When at last he walked across to her house, he was shown, by right of his relationship, into her private apartment,—which even he could not fail to observe was prettily furnished and tastefully adorned. Flowers of every hue and shape—azaleas, hydrangeas, and roses—were arranged about it on stands in symmetrical confusion; while on the tables and sideboard was displayed a wealth of ancient bronzes, cracked china, and old enamel vases, which would have driven most collectors wild with excitement. The walls were hung with scrolls, on some of which celebrated caligraphists had inscribed sentences from the classics, which Chang did not very well understand; and on others, distant hills, dotted with temples and enlivened by waterfalls, were depicted by old masters. One cool and shady scene, representing two old men playing at chess on a mountain-top beneath a wide-spreading pine-tree, and attended by boys bearing pipes and flasks, which might possibly be supposed to contain tea, especially attracted his attention; and so absorbed was he in the contemplation of it, that he was quite unaware that an even more attractive object had entered the room. Plum-blossom, for so the new arrival was named, seemed at first indisposed to interrupt her uncle's meditation, and stood watching him, holding the door in her hand. She had evidently attired herself with some care. Her hair was trimly arranged in a bunch on each side, after the manner of maidens; while a short fringe drooped over her forehead, which was both high and broad. Her silken robe hung in graceful folds over her plaited satin petticoat, from beneath which her small embroidered shoes obtruded their toes. In figure she was tall; and her features, which were fine and sharply marked, told a tale of high breeding and intelligence. Her eyes were large and well opened, and paid their tribute to her race by being slightly drawn up towards the outside corners. Her complexion needed neither powder nor rouge to add to its beauty; and the expression of her countenance generally was bright and mobile. Even Chang, when

"HE WAS QUITE UNAWARE THAT AN EVEN MORE ATTRACTIVE OBJECT HAD ENTERED THE ROOM."

she advanced to meet him, rose to greet her with admiring cordiality.

After the first compliments were over, Chang proceeded to open the object of his visit. "You are aware, my niece," said he, "how much your future has been in my mind since your father has been engaged in his present distant and doubtful service. I need not remind you of the saying of Mencius, that 'when a boy is born, the desire of his parents is that he may found a household; and from the time a girl appears in the world, the main object of her parents is to see her married;' nor need I go on to quote to you the sage's disapproval of all such who so far forsake the right path as to bore holes in partition walls and peep behind screens to catch glimpses of persons of the other sex" (this was a stab at Mr Iron). "Now, as I cannot but regard myself in the light of your father, I feel it incumbent on me to urge you to give your consent to be betrothed. I have made inquiries as to the young men of equal rank with yourself in the district, and with one consent my informants join in extolling the young Mr Wang, of whom I have before spoken to you, as being in every way a carp among minnows and a phœnix among magpies."

"If the minnows are drunkards and magpies *roués*, that is true enough," muttered Violet, Plum-blossom's attendant maiden, who, standing behind her mistress's chair, had listened with ill-concealed disgust to Chang's address. Fortunately Chang's senses were not very acute, and the interpolation was unnoticed by him.

"But, uncle," answered Plum-blossom, "though it

is true that my father is engaged on a distant mission, and that I have not heard from him for a long time, yet I have no right to assume either that he is dead—which may the Fates forbid—or that he may not at any moment return; and according to the 'Book of Rites,' it is the father who should betroth his daughter. My obvious duty is therefore to wait until I hear something definite either from him or of him."

"What you say is perfectly true in a general way," said Chang; "but even the sages acknowledged that, under certain circumstances, it was allowable, and sometimes even necessary, to depart from the common usage. Now yours is a case where such a departure is plainly called for. I have talked over the matter with the Prefect," added Chang, with some slight embarrassment, "and he is entirely of my opinion."

"That certainly adds weight to your arguments," answered Plum-blossom, demurely; "for though I have no personal knowledge of the Prefect, I have repeatedly heard of his fame as a man of wisdom and uprightness. So I will go as far as to say, uncle, that if you choose to act in all respects a father's part in this matter, I will give my consent. But, tell me, have you spoken on the subject to the young gentleman himself? I hope you have not been paying me compliments behind my back."

"I have spoken to him several times about the match," replied Chang; "but I should no more think of attempting to compliment you, as you say, than I should try to whiten a cloth washed in the waters of the Han or Keang and bleached in the sun. And, let me tell you, your good sense was never more apparent than at this moment. I felt convinced that a girl of your perception and wisdom would fall into the proposal which I, wholly and entirely in your interest, have so repeatedly made you. And now you know there will be a number of arrangements to be made," said Chang, determined to strike while the iron was hot; "and first of all, you must send to your future husband the eight characters representing the year, month, day, and hour of your birth, that they may be submitted to the fortune-teller."

"But already, uncle," said Plum-blossom, "you are breaking your agreement; and remember, if you break yours I may break mine. You undertook to act the part of a father to me, and it is therefore for you to send the *Pă-tsze*" (eight characters).

"You may be quite sure that I shall not retreat from my engagement," replied Chang; "but that there may not be any mistake, I should like you to write me a draft of the characters, that I may send them to be copied in gold, and that," he added aside, "I may hold your own handwriting as evidence against you, if by any chance you should turn fickle and change your mind."

"Certainly;" and calling for paper and pencil, Plum-blossom wrote down eight cyclical characters, and presented them to her uncle.

"Oh, lady, what have you done?" exclaimed Violet, wringing her hands as the door closed on Chang; "if you only knew as much about that young Wang as I do, you would die sooner than marry him. He is a brawler, a drunkard, an opium-smoker, a——"

"Hush!" said her mistress; "perhaps I know more than you think I do. And now listen to what I say. Don't feel or express surprise at anything I say or do in this matter; and as to the outside world, keep your eyes and ears open, and your mouth shut."

The look of despair which had taken possession of Violet's quaint-looking features gradually gave way under the influence of these words to one of surprised bewilderment. Her narrow slits of eyes opened their widest as she gazed with a searching look on the features of her mistress. By degrees she appeared to gather comfort from her inspection, and she promised implicit obedience to the instructions given her.

In the house of Chang there was wild rejoicing over the event. Only Mrs Chang seemed to have any misgiving. "I cannot make the girl out," she said. "It was but the other day that she vowed and declared she would not listen to the match, and now, with scarcely a show of resistance, she gives way. I hope she won't change her mind again as suddenly."

"There is no danger of her doing that," replied her husband, "for I persuaded her to write out her natal characters with her own hand, and here is the paper;" and so saying, he drew from his sleeve the paper given him by Plum-blossom. "But," he added, "she insists that as I am acting in the place of her father in this matter, *I* must have the characters cut out in gold-leaf, and the cards prepared to send to the bride-groom. I should be quite willing to do this, but, as a matter of fact, I have not got the money by me to pay for them."

"Oh, Wang will find the money readily enough. Go round to him at once and ask for it, and a little more in addition; and when the cards are ready, our eldest son shall act as emissary to take them to the bridegroom. It was a clever thought to get her to put pen to paper."

Mrs Chang was right. Wang produced the money almost with eagerness, and signalised the subsequent appearance of young Chang with the card by a sumptuous feast. In due course, also, the bridegroom, having prepared numerous and costly wedding-gifts, sent word to Chang that on a given day he would "humbly venture to send his paltry offering" to the young lady's "princely mansion." On receipt of this gratifying intimation, Chang went in high spirits to warn his niece of the intended ceremony.

"My dear uncle," said the young lady, "in the absence of my father, and in this empty and dismantled house, I could not possibly receive the presents. It would be neither proper to do so, nor would it be respectful to young Mr Wang. As you were kind enough to send the wedding-card for me, the return presents should, as a matter of course, be carried to your house; and besides, I cannot help feeling that as you have undertaken so much expense on my behalf, it is only fair that the presents, whatever they may be worth, should belong to you."

"Your wisdom and discretion really astonish me," said Chang, who could scarcely conceal his delight at the prospect of turning the presents into gold; "but while assenting, on the ground of propriety, to the arrangement you propose, I think the card of thanks had better be in your handwriting."

"Certainly," said Plum-blossom; "but it must of course run in your name, as it would have done in my father's name had he been here."

So saying, she sat down and inscribed a card of thanks. "There, I think that will do. Listen to what I have written: 'Chang Teming bows his head in acknowledgment of the wedding-presents sent to his daughter.'"

"Why put 'his daughter'?" objected Chang, doubtingly. "Young Wang is not going to marry my poor ugly daughter,—I wish he were; it is you, my niece."

"But as you have, with so much kindness and disinterestedness, taken upon yourself the part of a father towards me, it follows that I must be your daughter. To call yourself 'my father,' and me 'your niece,' would make people laugh and wonder."

"Very well, be it as you will," rejoined Chang, overcome by Plum-blossom's logic.

The new view proposed by his niece as to the ownership of the presents gave Chang an additionally keen interest in their arrival and value; and certainly nothing on the score of costliness could have been more gratifying to him than they were. So soon as he had carefully arranged them with his own hands in the family hall, he invited Plum-blossom over to inspect them. She expressed admiration at the taste shown in their choice, and at their great intrinsic value, and congratulated her uncle on their acquisition, adding, at the same time, that as she had no brother, the bulk of the family property would, she supposed, like these presents, pass into his possession.

"But whatever happens," said Chang, with a wave of his hand as though all such sordid ideas were abhorrent to him, "remember I shall always consider you as a daughter, and hope that you will in the same way look upon me in the light of a father."

If Chang had observed closely his niece's face as he spoke, he would have seen an expression of suppressed amusement, which might either have suggested to him the possibility that she had doubts on the subject of his disinterestedness, or given him reason to suspect that some scheme lurked beneath her seemingly extremely yielding demeanour. But his mind was just then so full of the prospect of freedom from debt, and of large perquisites, that such a trivial matter as his niece's face was obviously beneath his notice.

To young Wang the favourable turn which affairs had taken was an unfailing source of delight, and was marred only by the enforced exercise of patience required by the astrologer, who, after comparing the ticket of nativity sent by Chang with that of the intending bridegroom, had pronounced that the 15th of the next month was the date prescribed by fortune for the nuptials. At last the fateful day arrived, as all days will, however long waited for; and at early morn the impatient bridegroom sent his best-man to Chang to announce that on that same evening he should come to claim his bride. Chang could scarcely restrain his impatience sufficiently to perform properly the duties of a host to the welcome emissary; and no sooner had that young gentleman executed his last bow outside the front door, than his entertainer hurried over to Plum-blossom to warn her of the bridegroom's intended arrival. Demurely the young lady listened to her uncle's excited congratulations, and with an expression of assumed unconsciousness on her uplifted face, replied—

"But, my dear uncle, although I am profoundly interested in the future welfare of my cousin, Autumn-leaf, yet you can hardly expect me, I am sure, in my present condition of doubt as to my father's whereabouts, and even his life, to appear at the wedding; and I am at a loss, therefore, to understand why you, who must have so much to do, should have thought it necessary to inform me in such haste of the coming event."

Surprise, doubt, fear, and anger coursed in turn across Chang's features as these words fell upon his confused ears; and when his niece ceased to speak, all four sensations found full expression both in his countenance and voice.

"What do you mean," he hissed out, "by speaking of my daughter's marriage? Are you joking, or are you trying to play me false? It is you that young Wang is coming to marry, and it is you he shall marry this very night."

"My dear uncle, you are strangely inconsistent in this matter. If you will take the trouble to think, you will recollect that the wedding-cards were made out in the name of 'your daughter,' and that when the presents arrived at your house—not at mine, remember, uncle—you returned thanks for 'your daughter.' It is plain, then, that my cousin was the intended bride; for had you meant me, you would have spoken of me as your 'youngest daughter,' or 'adopted daughter'; but there was no such qualification, was there, uncle? I can assure you, also, that I have no present intention of marrying, and least of all marrying such a man as Wang, who, though he enjoys the benefit of your friendship, would hardly, I fear, prove a congenial companion to me." Plum-blossom could not deny herself this Parthian shot.

Chang listened like one thunder-struck; then springing from his chair, he paced up and down the room with long strides, giving vent to his passion in violent and most unoriental gesticulations.

"You deceitful wretch!" he cried, "do you suppose that I am going to be cheated and outraged by an ignorant young girl like you? I'll *make* you marry Wang; and," he added, as a sudden thought struck him, "though you may think yourself very clever, you have forgotten that you have left an evidence in my hand of your consent to the match. A murderer, you know, ought to destroy his weapon, and a thief should hide his crowbar; but you have given me, in your own handwriting, the evidence against you. I have only to produce your autograph-ticket of nativity before the Prefect, and he would order you to fulfil the contract."

This last retort Chang expected would have silenced Plum-blossom, or at least disconcerted her, but her outward calm was unruffled.

"Your answer would be complete, uncle," she replied, with almost a smile, "but for one small circumstance, which, strangely enough, you appear to have overlooked. The cyclical characters on the ticket represented the year, month, day, and hour of my cousin's birth, not mine."

The sound of a chuckle of suppressed laughter from behind the door where Violet was hidden, was interrupted by a vehement outburst from Chang.

"You lie!" he shouted; "and I will prove it." So saying, he burst out of the room so suddenly that he nearly knocked down Violet, who was in the act of peeping round the corner to watch the effect of her mistress's words.

"*He burst out of the room.*"

"Oh, my lady!" she exclaimed, as Chang's retreating figure disappeared, "how could you be so calm and quiet when he was raging so?"

"Because," replied Plum-blossom, "I had him in the palm of my hand, being conscious of my own integrity and of his evil intentions. Don't you remember how Confucius played a tune on his lyre when he and his disciples were attacked by banditti? And if he could show such indifference to danger in circumstances of so great peril, should not I be able to preserve a calm demeanour in the presence of this storming bully?"

The sound of Chang's returning footsteps drove Violet again into her place of concealment. "There," he said as he entered the room, "is the paper you gave me; and now deny your own handwriting if you dare."

"Please sit down, uncle, and let me ask you one or two questions. What was the date of my birth?"

"You were born on the 15th of the 8th month, in the second watch. I and your father were, as it happened, drinking to the full moon when the news was brought us."

"And when did your daughter, Autumn-leaf, first see the light?"

"On the 6th of the 6th month, as I well remember; for the weather was so intensely hot that her mother's life was in danger."

"And now, uncle, will you read the date represented by the cyclical characters on the paper which you hold in your hand?"

"Oh, I don't know anything about cyclical characters," replied Chang. "Such knowledge," he added in a vain attempt to conceal his ignorance, "is only fit for astrologers and women."

"Is it possible," said Plum-blossom, in a tone of revengeful mockery, "that, with your wide circle of knowledge, you don't understand these simple characters? Well then, let me, 'ignorant young girl' as I am, explain them to you. These first characters, *Ke wei*, stand for the month which is vulgarly known as the Serpent month, which, as perhaps you know, is the sixth month."

"Yes, I know that."

"Well, these next characters, *Keă yin*, represent the sixth day of the month, and this is, therefore, the date of my cousin's birth, and not of mine—the year of our births being the same."

"You have attempted to ruin me," he said, "by an abominable fraud; but I will be even with you. I will impeach you before the Prefect, and then see whether you will be able to escape from the clutches of the law as easily as you think you have from mine."

"You had better not be in too great a hurry, uncle. From things I have lately heard, the Prefect has not been altogether acting with you in this matter; and if I were to charge you with attempting to decoy me into a marriage in the absence of my father and against my consent, it might go hardly with you."

"What does it matter?" groaned the wretched man, as he threw himself back in his chair; "I am ruined, whatever happens. So what can I do better than either throw myself into the well or take a dose of gold-leaf, and so end my miseries?"

"I have a better plan than either of those you suggest," said Plum-blossom; "and if you will listen to my advice, I think I can get you out of your difficulty. You would like to have your daughter married, I suppose?"

"Does not a weary man long to throw his burden off his back?"

"Very well, then, why should you not throw this burden into the lap of young Wang? He has throughout the business negotiated for 'your daughter'; then let him take your daughter."

"But he will discover the fraud."

"Not until it is too late. He won't see her face until she is his wife, and then he will be ashamed to confess that he has been hoodwinked."

"Well," said Chang, after a few minutes' reflection, "as it is the only way out of the difficulty, I will risk it. But there is no time to be lost; and the least you can do, after the way you have behaved, is to come over and help us with the arrangements, for young Wang is to be here this evening."

Peace being thus restored, the unnatural allies went to propose their scheme to Autumn-leaf. That young lady, who was as free from any bashfulness or refined feeling as her worthy parent, was delighted at the idea. Being very plain in appearance and ungainly in figure, she had entertained but faint hopes of matrimony, and the prospect, therefore, of gaining a husband so rich as young Wang was charming beyond measure to her. She at once consented to play the part required, and, without a moment's loss of time, prepared to bedeck herself for the occasion. Anticipating the marriage, Chang had arranged everything in readiness except the bride. The decorations and scarlet hangings were all at hand, and a very few hours' work sufficed to adorn the family hall and altar with the splendours usual on such occasions. But the bride was not so easily beautified. However, after all the resources of Plum-blossom's wardrobe, as well as her own, had been exhausted in choosing dresses and petticoats which became her best, she was pronounced presentable. Much the confederates trusted to the long red veil which was to cover her face and person until her arrival at her new home; and minute were the directions which Plum-blossom gave her for concealing her features until the next morning.

"Assume a modesty, even if you don't feel bashful. Shrink within the curtains when your husband approaches you, and protest against his keeping the lamp alight. If in the morning there should be an outbreak of anger on his part, try to soften him with tears; and if that should prove unavailing, pretend to be in despair and threaten suicide. No man likes a fuss and a scandal; and after a time, you may be quite sure he will settle down quietly."

Primed with this excellent advice, Autumn-leaf went through the ceremonies of the day without betraying herself. The awkwardness with which she entered the audience-hall and bowed to the bridegroom was put down by himself and his friends to natural timidity. The remaining rites she executed faultlessly. She did reverence to heaven and earth and to her ancestors, and finally entered the bridal sedan-chair which was to carry her to her new home with complete composure, much to the relief of her father, who all day long was so tremulous with nervous excitement, that, from time to time, he was compelled to seek courage from his opium-pipe.

"She was pronounced presentable."

When at last the doors were shut on the bridal pair his gratification was great, although, at the same time, it was painfully mingled with a sense of the possible evil consequences which might very likely ensue on the course he had taken. However, for the present there was freedom from anxiety, and he wisely determined to let the future take care of itself.

"I should like to see Mr Wang's face when he wakes to-morrow morning," said Violet, laughing, as she followed her mistress back to her apartments. "But," she added, as the sound of loud raps were heard at the front door, "who can that be knocking at the street gate so violently? He cannot, surely, have found out the trick already? If he has, what *will* you do?"

The first question was soon answered, for just as she finished speaking, a servant announced that the Prefect had sent his secretary to inquire whether Plum-blossom's marriage, which he had only just heard was in course of performance, was taking place with her full consent or not, as he was prepared to interfere in case she was being coerced; and at the same time to hand her a letter from her father which had been forwarded with the usual official despatches from Peking.

"Beg the secretary to assure the Prefect," replied Plum-blossom, "that his infinite kindness towards me is deeply engraven on my heart; and to inform him that, happily for me, it was not I who was married this evening but my cousin."

With impatience and deep emotion Plum-blossom

now turned to open her father's letter, the contents of which brought tears of delight to her eyes, and caused Violet to perform a dance as nearly resembling a fandango as is possible, with feet just two inches and a half long. That the President should have returned from the frontier covered with honours was only what Plum-blossom felt might have been looked for; but that he expected to arrive at Ping-chow on the very next day, was a cause of unspeakable joy and relief to her. This, however, was not quite all the news the letter contained. "I am bringing with me," wrote her father, "a young Mr Tieh, to whose foresight and courage I mainly attribute the successful issue of my mission."

WITHIN HIS DANGER.

"You stand within his danger, do you not?"
—*Merchant of Venice.*

IT was a common saying among the ancients that he who had visited Hang-chow had been to the City of Heaven. The modern Chinaman, breathing the same enthusiastic admiration for the most beautiful city in Eastern Asia, says, "See Hang-chow and die;" and unless we are to suppose that every traveller who has visited the town has been a victim to hallucinations, there are few spots on the surface of the earth which surpass in bright beauty the city and neighbourhood of Hang-chow. Earth, sky, and water there combine to form one of the most lovely pieces of landscape-gardening on a gigantic scale that it is possible to imagine; while the coloured roofs of the *yamun* and pagodas, the countless bridges and splendid temples of the city, present objects of man's art which are not unworthy of their natural environments. Even the wondrous beauty of the lake which washes the western wall of the city, is held to be heightened by the temples, palaces, and pavilions which adorn the islands scattered over its surface; while all around it are erected beautiful palaces and mansions, of the richest and most exquisite structure.

On summer evenings it is the habit of these noble citizens to take their pleasure on the lake in barges, which reflect in their bright decorations and luxurious fittings the meretricious beauty of their surroundings. In such a galley, one glorious evening in early autumn, the magistrate of Hang-chow was taking his ease at the close of a hard day's work, and by contact with the fresh breezes of heaven, was seeking to rid himself of the taint of chicanery, bribery, and intrigue which infected every nook and corner of his *yamun.* His *compagnon de voyage* was a Mr Tso, an old resident at Hang-chow, and one in whose judgment the magistrate placed much confidence. Being rich and independent, he could afford to hold his own opinions, even when they clashed with those of his present host; and accustomed as the magistrate was to the society of toadies, it was refreshing to find a man who did not hesitate to contradict him to his face. The evening was one rather for still enjoyment than for much talking, and for some minutes not a word had been spoken between the friends, when, on rounding a point in the lake, the boat sailed into view of the house and grounds, famed in local history as being the most beautiful among the beautiful, and as having descended in the Ts'êng family from father to son through countless generations.

" Well," said the magistrate, after gazing long and admiringly at the landscape, " if I were not the magistrate of Hang-chow, I would be Mr Ts'êng. What an enviable lot his is !—young, rich, talented, the husband of a charming wife, if report speaks truly, and the owner of such a lovely house and gardens as those yonder. That willow clump is just the spot where Su Tungp'o would have loved to have written sonnets; and that mass of waving colour is enough to make Tsau Fuhing rise from his grave and seize his paint-brush again."

"I don't deny," replied Mr Tso, "that Ts'êng's lot has fallen to him in pleasant places. But though I should much like to exchange possessions with him, nothing would induce me to exchange personalities. He never seems really happy. His is one of those timid and fearful natures which are always either in the depths of misery or in the highest of spirits. He is so sensitive that the least thing disturbs him; and he is so dependent on outside influences, that a smile or a frown from Fortune either makes or mars him. And then, between ourselves, I have my doubts as to his scholarship. It is true that he passed his B.A. examination with honours, but it did so happen that his uncle was the chief examiner on the occasion; and though I don't charge either uncle or nephew with anything underhand, yet my son tells me that others are not so charitable."

"You are all, I think, hard on our friend," said the magistrate. "I don't know much of him, but I have always heard him spoken of as a man of learning and ability. However, I have written to invite him to my picnic on the lake to-morrow, and we will then try him at verse-making, and see what he is really made of."

That the magistrate's admiration for the Ts'êng

gardens was fully justified, every admirer of brilliant colouring would readily admit. Indeed no fairer prospect could be imagined, and as the autumn sun sent its slanting rays through the waving branches of the willows and oaks, and added lustre to the blood-red leaves of the maples, it was difficult to suppose that anything but peace and content could reign in so lovely a spot.

But Tso was not far wrong in his estimate of Ts'êng's character; and in addition to the bar to happiness presented by its infirmities, there was one dire misfortune which took much of the brightness out of his life. Though he had been married six years he had but one child, and that a daughter. It was true that he was devotedly fond of the little Primrose, as he called her, but nothing could make up to him for the failure of a son to carry on the succession of his name and fortune, and to continue the worship at the family graves.

At the very moment that the magistrate and his friend were passing down the lake, Ts'êng and his wife, Golden-lilies, were sitting in a pavilion, which stood in the midst of the flower-garden, surrounded by a profusion of blue hydrangeas, China asters, pomegranates, citrons, jasmines, peonias, honeysuckles, and other flowers indigenous to the favoured regions of Central China, watching Primrose chasing a curly-coated puppy along the crooked paths as well as her poor little cramped feet would allow her, and trying to catch the leaves which were beginning to sprinkle the earth with specks of every hue; and they were still so employed when a servant handed a letter to Ts'êng, who, recognising from the envelope that it was from the magistrate, opened it with an expression of nervous anxiety. His trepidation, however, turned into pleasure, as he read as follows :—

"With great respect I beg to invite you to-morrow at noon to the still clear waters of immeasurable depth, to enjoy the delights of poetry and the wine-cup. As our galley shall glide through the crystal waves of the lake, we will watch the floating leaves strike her gentle sides ; and when we have exhausted our songs, and drained the cup of our delights, we will turn our prow towards the shore."

This invitation was one of those smiles of fortune which had a strangely exhilarating effect on Ts'êng's variable temperament, and he hurried off to his study in the highest spirits to accept it.

"Reverently," he wrote, "I return answer to your jade-like epistle. What can surpass the calm beauty of the lake by moonlight or the tragic aspect of its waves in storm and rain? Your honour having deigned to command my presence on your stately boat, I, as in duty bound, will seize whip to follow you. My paltry literary attainments you will, I fear, find infinitely deficient ; and I am much afraid that I shall weary you with my efforts to express in verse my admiration for the mountains and lake."

The day of the magistrate's picnic opened bright and fine, and with commendable punctuality Ts'êng and his fellow-guests assembled at the landing-place, to which usually dreary spot their silk and satin robes and highly coloured skull-caps gave an unwonted air of gaiety. The last to arrive was the host, who, on dismounting from his sedan, bowed collectively and repeatedly to his friends, lifting his joined hands to his forehead as if in supplication, and then bending low in an attitude of humble adoration. His twelve guests returned his salutation with supple knees and effusive tokens of respect. These ceremonies accomplished, the whole party embarked on the barge. The vessel was one of the best of its kind, but was not a bark to brook a mighty sea. The two masts were innocent of sails, and were burdened only with flags, setting forth in large character the rank and titles of the magistrate. The forepart was decked over, and formed the abode night and day of the crew. Abaft this forecastle was an open space, extending to midships, where arose a large and luxuriously furnished deck-house. The window-frames were prettily painted and adorned with wood-carving, while at the portal were suspended painted-glass lanterns, from which hung fringes and tassels. Inside, chairs, tables, and a divan afforded abundant accommodation; and round the room were ranged stands on which stood rare and curiously trained plants in costly porcelain pots.

At the word *K'aich'uen* ("unmoor the ship"), given by the magistrate, the crew, with the help of a crowd of idlers on the wharf, launched the vessel into the deep. The island to which they were bound was about a mile from the shore, and thitherwards the crew, with that happy absence of all signs of hurry which belongs to us orientals, impelled the craft by slow and deliberate strokes of their long sweeping oars. On landing, the magistrate led the way to a Buddhist temple which stood on a platform of rocks overlooking the lake. No more appropriate spot could possibly have been chosen for the occasion. The view over the still waters of the lake, dotted here and there with verdure-clad islets of every shape, was indescribably beautiful; and the temple, which in its arrangements and adornments resembled rather a temple of the god of pleasure than of the ascetic Buddha, supplied all that was necessary to minister to the wants of the magistrate and his friends.

With the help of the priests the feast was quickly spread, and with sharpened appetites the guests sat down to the excellent cheer provided for them. Merrily the wine went round, and under its influence Ts'êng's spirits, which had been encouraged by the marked attention shown him by the magistrate and Tso, rose considerably. Even the proposition, ingeniously made by Tso towards the end of the feast, that they should amuse themselves by verse-making, had only a slightly depressing effect upon him. At any other time the thought of having to submit extempore compositions to the criticism of twelve judges would have reduced him to trembling fear; but now, as the themes were given out, he seized his pencil and hazarded stanzas which, though they saved him from the accustomed penalty of drinking off three cups of wine, brought the magistrate rapidly round to Tso's estimate of his literary ability.

But the significant glances which were exchanged between the two observant friends were quite lost upon Ts'êng, who talked more and laughed louder than anybody else; and finally, on their return, he made his adieux to his host and companions, and turned homewards flattered and self-satisfied. The night, for it was late, was fine and warm, and as he sauntered on his way, he recalled with pleasure the compliments which had been paid him and the smart things he had said. As he approached his house, however, these grateful cogitations were interrupted by the sound of angry voices, which, on advancing, he perceived were centred at his own doorway. His presence produced a momentary lull in the storm of angry abuse.

"What is all this about?" he demanded, rather for something to say than for the sake of information: for, as a matter of fact, the voices of the disputants had been so high that he was already fully aware of the cause of quarrel between two of his servants, Tan and Le, and an old pedlar, who now stood breathless with passion before him.

"The matter, your honour! Why, this old rogue wants to cheat us out of a hundred cash for these two trumpery rice-bowls, the like of which we could buy anywhere for fifty!"

"May your words choke you, you idle, good-for-nothing vagabonds!" shouted the old man, trembling with anger, and shaking his fist at the speaker. "Eighty cash I gave for them at Su-chow; and after having carried them on my bamboo all these miles, am I to sell them to you for less than they cost me?"

At any other time Ts'êng would have avoided all participation in the quarrel, and would probably have hastened to put himself beyond the reach of the angry voices. But the magistrate's wine was still potent in him, and he felt disposed to let his servants see that when he was so minded he could face even so formidable an adversary as an angry old pedlar.

"I cannot have you making such a disturbance at my door," he said, with a motion of the hand, which was meant to be haughty; "nor can I have my servants abused by a man like you. So be off, and take the price they offer you for the bowls."

But the waves of the old man's wrath were too high to be stilled by a word from Ts'êng, and he turned fiercely on that young gentleman—

"Who are you," he cried, "that you should tell me what to take and what to leave? Because you got a degree through your uncle's favouritism, you think yourself entitled to dictate to me, do you? Nay, don't pretend to be angry; you know what I say is true, and other people know it also. Did I not hear young Mr Liu charge you with it in the street of Longevity the other day? and did I not see you, instead of facing him, sneak away like a whipped cur?"

The greater the truth the more bitter the sting. The pedlar's words cut Ts'êng like a whip, and the anger which rose in his breast being supported by his borrowed courage, he seized the old man by the throat, and with a violent shove threw him backwards on the pathway. Having accomplished this heroic feat, he turned to his servants with an expression which said plainly, "See what I can do when I am really roused."

"THREW HIM BACKWARDS ON THE PATHWAY."

Catching his cue, the servants assumed attitudes of astonished admiration.

"Hai-yah," said one, "your honour's anger is more terrible than a lion's rage!"

"If he had only known the measure of your honour's courage," said the other, "he would have mounted a tiger's back rather than anger you."

Pleased and triumphant, Ts'êng turned to take another look at his fallen victim, when, to his horror and alarm, he saw him lying silent, motionless, and death-like on the spot where he had fallen. Instantly his assumed air of braggadocio left him, the blood fled from his flushed cheeks, and in the twinkling of an eye there passed through his mind a vision of himself branded as a murderer, carried before the magistrate, imprisoned, tortured, and beheaded. The vision, momentary though it was, was enough to rack his nervous temperament with fearful terrors; and forgetful of his former attitude, he threw himself on the ground by the prostrate pedlar, imploring him to rouse himself, and calling on his servants to help him raise the apparently lifeless man.

But the servants were nearly as unnerved as their master; and it was with great difficulty that the three men carried their victim into the doorkeeper's room. There Golden-lilies, who had been disturbed by the noise, found the three men helplessly gazing at the senseless form of the old man. Hastily sending one servant for cold water, and another for a fan, she took her place by the bedside, and having unfastened the pedlar's collar, turned to her husband to ask an explanation of the affair. As well as his confused mind would let him, he told his story with tolerable accuracy. Only in one place did he kick over the traces of truth, and that was when he roundly asserted that he had not used violence towards the sufferer. "I merely," said he, "laid my hand upon his shoulder, and it was while starting back in a nervous tremor that his foot slipped on the pavement and down he fell." To the servants who had now returned Ts'êng appealed for confirmation of this statement, and received from them a warm verbal support of this very new story; alas! how different a one from that in which he had gloried but a few moments before!

Meanwhile Golden-lilies was sprinkling the old man's face with the water, and gently fanning him, in response to which judicious treatment he opened his eyes. At first his gaze was strange and wild, but presently he recognised those about him; and to Ts'êng's infinite relief, asked where he was, and what had happened. Returning consciousness gave life to his formerly death-like features, and the recognition of it produced a no less change in Ts'êng's countenance. The vision which had passed through his mind when he thought the old man was dead, had haunted him still, and no effort would prevent the pictures his imagination had conjured up from returning to his mental sight. Now he could thrust them on one side as a man throws off a nightmare; and in his delight he seized the awakened pedlar's hand, and would have shaken it wildly had not Golden-lilies warned him to do nothing of the kind. By degrees the old man recovered his recollection of all that had passed; and when a cup of tea had still further revived him, Ts'êng led him to the divan in the reception-hall, while wine was warmed for his benefit. Again and again Ts'êng expressed his regret at the accident; and when the old man insisted on starting homewards, lest he should be too late for the ferry-boat across the lake, his host presented him, as a peace-offering, with two ounces of silver and a roll of silk, neatly packed away in one of Golden-lilies' baskets. When the door was closed on his guest, Ts'êng betook himself to Golden-lilies' apartments with an intense feeling of relief. His mind was incapable of perspective; and in all affairs of life the present loomed so large to his mental sight, that everything else was invisible. At this moment his escape from a great peril gave a nervous elasticity to his spirits which contrasted painfully with his abject dejection of a few hours before. Golden-lilies, rightly divining the frame of mind in which he was likely to be, had prepared for him a soothing repast of chicken's liver, sweetmeats, and *ginseng*, with a pot of some excellent Su-chow wine to wash them down. Though not hungry, Ts'êng was feverish and thirsty, and the quantity of wine he took was quite out of proportion to the quantity of viands he ate. However, Golden-lilies' end was attained. He was revived and strengthened, and she even did not object to his becoming somewhat excited. It was better than seeing him leaden-eyed and trembling. By degrees, under the influence of the wine, he began to explain away the slip which he had been so glad to invent to account for the pedlar's fall, and was just describing the pot-valiant part he had played, when Tan hurriedly entered with the news that Lai, the ferryman, was outside, and insisted on seeing his honour at once. The man's face and manner were so perturbed that all the beneficial effects of Golden-lilies' feast vanished, and she turned to see her lord and master again pale and limp.

"What is the matter?" asked Ts'êng, as the ferryman, without waiting for an invitation, entered the room. This man was one of Ts'êng's many *bêtes-noires.* He was a rough, determined fellow, with a truculent face, and a no less truculent manner. He had, further, an unconcealed contempt for Ts'êng, and lost no opportunities of showing it. That this man, therefore, should be the bearer of what Ts'êng instinctively knew to be bad tidings, was an additional bitterness to the pill.

"I have brought you bad news, Mr Ts'êng, and thought I would just step in and tell you, before going on to the magistrate," added the man, ominously.

"What is your news?" said Ts'êng, in vain attempting to suppress his apprehensions.

"The old pedlar, Ting, whom you threw down on the pavement, is dead."

If the executioner's axe had at that moment descended on the neck of poor Ts'êng, he could not have looked more bereft of life than he did as he threw himself back in his chair at these words. For some seconds his power of speech failed him, and at last he gasped out—

"What do you mean? How did he die? Not that it matters to me," he added, with a violent effort to appear calm.

"He came down to my boat to cross the lake," said Lai, looking steadfastly on his victim, "and after we had gone a short way across he appeared to turn faint and giddy, and at last he tumbled off the seat into the bottom of the boat. As quickly as I could I put down my oars to help him up, when I saw it was something worse than a faint, and he had just time to tell me of the scuffle at your door, and that you had pushed him down and killed him, when he fell back dead."

"It is a lie," screamed Ts'êng; "when he left this house he was quite well."

"Well, all I know is," said Lai, "that he is now dead, and that when in the act of death he said you were his murderer. These are some things," he added, holding up Golden-lilies' basket with the roll of silk, "which he had in his hand when he came into the boat."

Ts'êng gazed at these evidences of the truth of the man's story with a fixed and glassy stare, while poor Golden-lilies stood by with her face in her hands weeping bitterly. In one short day all that had been pleasurable in their existence had been exchanged for blank despair. The morning had opened with bright hopes and brilliant expectations, and now the evening had set in with a black darkness of misery which crushed them to the ground. For some seconds not another word was uttered. But presently Golden-lilies went over to her husband, and taking his hand in hers, whispered something in his ear, which brought a ray of intelligence into his face.

"Yes, you are right; I will try," he faltered.

"You and I have known one another a long time, Lai," he said, "and I am sure you would not do an injury to an old neighbour and friend. This is a bad business, and I swear to you I am not to blame. His foot slipped and he fell down. It will do you no good to tell any one about it; and if you will keep the secret, I will willingly pay you handsomely. Oh, promise me that you will," said the wretched man, throwing himself at Lai's feet.

"Here was a pretty position for a graduate and an expectant mandarin!"

Here was a pretty position for a graduate and an expectant mandarin! On his knees at the feet of a common fellow, who did not know one character from another, and who knew as much about Confucius as he did about the Book of Changes!

"Well, Mr Ts'êng," said Lai, "I don't want to do anything to injure you, but the man died in my boat; so that unless I can explain his death, I shall be charged with the murder."

"Where is he?" gasped poor Ts'êng.

"In my boat," said Lai. "I have anchored it in a quiet place up the river, so that no one should go on board."

"Oh, if you will only keep the matter a secret," said Ts'êng, rising as his hopes rose, "I will give you any sum you ask."

"But what am I to do with the body?" hesitated Lai.

"You can bury it in my graveyard, which is, as you know, on the bank of the lake. The night is very dark, and the wall round the yard is high, so that no one will see you."

"But I cannot do it by myself."

"No; but I will send two of my servants with you. If you will only do this for me, I will be your slave for the rest of my life."

"Well," said Lai, after a few moments' apparent consideration, "if you will give me money enough to set up a fish-shop, I don't mind doing this job to oblige you."

"Gladly I will," said Ts'êng; "and now I will call the servants." So having summoned Tan and Le, he repeated to them the story told by Lai. With many appeals to their good feeling and sense of gratitude, he begged them to do him this service, promising that he would give them substantial rewards if they consented. After some hesitation and discussion, the men came to terms, and went off with the ferryman, armed with spades.

The three men stole out like conspirators into the street, and, following devious lanes and unfrequented ways, they reached the boat, snugly moored under the bank of the lake.

"Take care where you go," said Lai, as they stepped on board, "and just sit where you are while I get to the oars." The men, who were beginning to feel nervous and frightened, needed no second bidding; and after half an hour's pull, Lai, who knew the lake as well by night as by day, ran the boat ashore at Ts'êng's family graveyard.

"Now come here and help me with the old man," said he, as soon as he had secured the boat to the bank.

"Why, he is all wet," said Tan, as he helped to lift the body.

"I know," answered Lai; "he fell into the water when he turned giddy, and I had to pull him out."

"You did not say anything about that up at the house," said Tan.

"Well, I tell you now, and that is enough, is it not?" answered Lai, sullenly.

With considerable difficulty the three men groped their way into the graveyard bearing their ghastly burden, and at once set to work to dig a grave. Every now and then the sound of passing footsteps made them pause in their work; and once they were evidently heard, for through the darkness there came the challenge—"Who is that in Mr Ts'êng's graveyard?" But presently the challenger went on, and before long the dead body was safely laid to rest, and the soil beaten flat over it. So soon as the work was done, the men made their way hastily to the boat, being glad enough to escape from the dark, silent, and ghostly cemetery. On their return they found Ts'êng anxiously awaiting them. Again and again he made them assure him that no one had seen them, and as often he made them swear that they would keep his secret faithfully. That night the two servants went to bed rich men, while Ts'êng retired to Golden-lilies' apartment to try to lose his consciousness of misery in sleep. But this was beyond his power; occasionally he dosed, but only to dream that the pedlar was standing in the street accusing him aloud of his murder, and then with a violent start and scream he awoke. Poor Golden-lilies fared very little better; and when morning dawned they both arose, weary and unrefreshed, to meet they knew not what, and to face their difficulties with the best courage they could muster.

The sight even of the two confederate servants was a torture to poor Ts'êng, who knew, or fancied he knew, that they were watching him to see how a murderer would behave himself, and were mentally speculating on what would happen if the secret they held in their possession ever became known. In the same way every incident which occurred bore reference in his imagination to the terrible event of the preceding evening. Even little Primrose's innocent questions of why he looked so pale, and why he would not come out with her into the garden as usual, were more than he could endure; and the child was promptly handed over to her nurse, who had orders to keep her quiet and at a distance. As to his being able to eat any breakfast, that was quite out of the question; and if there had been any chance of his having an appetite for dinner, it was dissipated by a note he received from a neighbour, who wrote to say, that in passing the Ts'êng cemetery on the preceding night he had heard the sound of pickaxes and shovels, and that to his question of "Who was there?" he had failed to get a reply. The writer excused himself for not having gone into the graveyard, by pleading the lateness of the hour and the darkness of the night. But he "humbly ventured to recommend that Ts'êng should look into the matter."

With a look of indescribable misery, Ts'êng handed this letter to Golden-lilies, who throughout the morning, partly, possibly, because hers was not the head in danger, had shown a much bolder front to fortune than her lord and master had been able to do, but also, doubtless, because, though of the softer sex, she was made of sterner stuff.

"Sit down and answer the letter at once," she said, "and, while thanking him for his vigilance" ("Curse him for it," muttered Ts'êng), "say that you will send at once to make inquiries."

Ts'êng did as he was bid, and then relapsed into blank misery. Possibly he was under the delusion that remorse for having taken the life of a fellow-creature was the mainspring of his mental agony; but had he analysed his feelings carefully, he would have found that that feeling hardly entered at all into his cogitations. Blank fear it was that oppressed him; fear of being dragged off to prison as a murderer—fear of having to face the magistrate who had so lately entertained him—fear of being tortured if he did not confess, and fear, if he did, of the executioner's fatal weapon. If he had been capable of diving into his inner feelings, he would have known that an assurance that his crime would never be discovered, had that been possible, would have lifted the whole weight from his over-burdened soul; but now, while at one moment in his terror he almost wished that it might be brought to light at once, that he might escape from his torturing suspense—at another, he tried to buoy himself up with the hope that it would never be found out. One thing he had determined to do, and that was, as soon as he had settled with Lai, who was to call after dusk, he would go himself to the graveyard to make quite sure that the work was well done. Much though he hated and feared the ferryman, he now had a morbid longing for his arrival; and when that worthy appeared, he received him with open arms.

Lai was as undemonstrative and self-possessed as Ts'êng was effusive and flurried; and a glance at that unfortunate young gentleman was enough to convince his visitor that he had the game in his hands.

"Well, Mr Ts'êng," he began, as he seated himself uninvited, "I have come according to arrangement to settle about last night's job."

"Yes, yes; don't say anything more about *that*," said Ts'êng, shuddering. "I have here two hundred taels of silver, which I hope you will accept from me."

"That is not enough," answered Lai; "do you think I would have buried a murdered man——"

"Oh don't, don't. Well, come, I will give you another fifty taels; surely that will satisfy you," said Ts'êng, who, though anxious to quiet Lai, had an intense dislike to parting with his money.

"Now, look here, Mr Ts'êng," said Lai deliberately, and with a threatening countenance, "if you don't give me down three hundred taels, good weight, I shall go on at once to the magistrate's to——"

"Say no more, you shall have the three hundred. And now, I have something to ask of you—I want you to row me up to the graveyard and show me where *it* is."

"Very well," replied Lai, "there will not be any one wanting to cross the lake to-night, so we can start now if you like."

"Is it dark enough?" asked Ts'êng.

"It is so dark that you might run into your best friend's arms without his knowing you; and unless you have the eyes of a cat or an owl, you won't see much when you get there."

With much caution the expedition was made, and Ts'êng satisfied himself, so far as the darkness would allow, that every care had been taken to make the newly made grave as much like the surrounding soil as possible. He returned, therefore, with his mind now at rest, and as days went by and nothing serious occurred to arouse his fears, he gradually recovered much of his ordinary placidity. Not that he altogether escaped annoyance; for Lai, luxuriating in his suddenly acquired wealth, showed a tendency to break out into riot, and in his cups he allowed himself to talk of his friendship with "young Ts'êng" in a way which, coupled with his sudden wealth, made his neighbours wonder and gossip. From some of these Ts'êng learnt what was going on. The bare idea of his alliance with Lai becoming a subject of tittle-tattle was torture to him, and he took an

"With much caution the expedition was made."

opportunity of begging the ferryman to be more cautious. Being not unwilling to worry poor Ts'êng, Lai affected to be indifferent to anything people might say, and adopted altogether so defiant a tone, that he brought Ts'êng once again to his knees.

To add to Ts'êng's anxieties, little Primrose was

seized one evening with a violent headache and every symptom of high fever. For three days the child lay tossing to and fro with burning skin, parched mouth, and throbbing head; and when, at the end of that time, these symptoms abated, their origin was made plain by an eruption which was unmistakably that of smallpox. The doctor who was summoned felt the pulse of the sufferer and prescribed *ginseng*, and broth made of cassia shoots, in accordance with the dictum of the highest authorities. But to this orthodox treatment the disease declined to submit. The virulence of the distemper was unchecked; and though Golden-lilies paid numerous visits to the shrine of the Goddess of Smallpox, and spent large sums of money in the purchase of offerings to that deity, the child daily and hourly grew worse, until the doctor had unwillingly to acknowledge that he could do nothing more. It is difficult to say which of the parents during these dark days suffered the greatest mental agony. Golden-lilies' distress was that of an agonised mother, tortured by the fear of losing her only child; while Ts'êng's grief at the possible loss of his fondling, was aggravated by a superstitious belief that his own crime had brought this misery upon him. Even the doctor, accustomed as he was to displays of affection, was touched by the grief of the young couple, and, forgetful of all professional etiquette, he recommended Ts'êng, as a last hope, to send for a quack practitioner, residing at a town some twenty miles away, who had, he said, acquired a reputation for the successful treatment of similar desperate cases.

Eagerly catching at this straw, Ts'êng wrote a note begging the doctor "to deign to visit his reed hut, and to bend his omniscient mind to the case of his insignificant child," and bade Tan carry it at once to its destination. But since the night when Ts'êng had been obliged to place his secret in the hands of his two servants, their manner had been less respectful than formerly, and sometimes even defiant. To Tan the present mission was evidently distasteful; and it was only by the promise of a handsome reward that Ts'êng at last succeeded in getting him off. During the whole afternoon of that day, time seemed to the watchers to stand still; and towards night, when they hoped that the expected doctor might appear, every approaching horse's hoof brought hope, which as often was destined to be disappointed as the tramp died away again in the distance. Meanwhile Primrose grew worse and worse. As night came on unconsciousness set in; and just before dawn the little thing gave a deep sigh and passed into the land of shades.

Both Ts'êng and Golden-lilies were completely crushed by the ruin of all their hopes; and when Tan made his appearance towards noon, they scarcely heeded his explanation that he had waited all night at the doctor's house, expecting his return from a distant professional visit, and that, when morning came, he had thought it best to come back, even without the doctor, to report his want of success.

Much sympathy was felt with the sorrow-stricken parents at the loss of their only child, and many were the visits of condolence which Ts'êng received during the ensuing days. Among others, a relation called, who, after having expressed his sympathy, added with evident reluctance—"There is a matter, my brother, about which I feel bound to speak to you, although I am most unwilling to trouble you about ordinary affairs at such a time as this."

"Please don't let my affliction interfere with any matter of business," said Ts'êng.

"Well, the fact is," said his guest, "that the other morning—it was, I remember, the morning when your little one departed for the 'Yellow Springs'—one of my servants came home very much the worse for wine and opium; and on my asking him for an explanation of his conduct, he said that a man of yours named Tan had kept him up all night drinking and smoking at an opium-tavern in the town. Can this be true?"

"It is quite impossible," replied Ts'êng; "for the whole of that night Tan was twenty miles away, at the house of a doctor to whom I had sent him."

"Well, I have brought my man," said the other, "that he may repeat his story in your presence, and that, if necessary, we should confront him with Tan."

"Let him come in, by all means," said Ts'êng.

In obedience to a summons Tan's accuser entered the room. He was a dissipated-looking fellow. His face was thin and drawn, and of that peculiar mahogany hue which is begotten by long-continued indulgence in the opium-pipe. From the same habit his teeth were blackened, and the whites of his eyes looked as though they had been smoke-dried. On entering he bowed his knee, and then proceeded to give a circumstantial account of the night in question. At first Ts'êng had treated his accusations with contempt; but the remarkably coherent manner in which the man retailed his story, suggested doubts to his mind, which tortured him with misgivings. Without waiting for the conclusion of the man's statement, therefore, he summoned Tan to face his accuser. With a glance Tan took in the position of affairs, and having with a considerable effort mastered the uneasiness which the crisis provoked, he stood ready to brazen it out.

"This man tells me," said Ts'êng, "that instead of carrying my letter to the doctor the other evening, you passed the night drinking and smoking with him at a tavern in the town. Is this true or false?"

"It is false, your honour; and I can only suppose that this man, to whom I have only spoken once or twice in my life, must have invented this story out of spite, or in order to shield, in some way which I do not understand, his own conduct from blame."

"Are not you ashamed to tell such a lie in the sight of heaven?" said the man, quite taken aback by the coolness of the denial; "but fortunately I have some evidence of the truth of my story, which you will find it hard to meet. Did you deliver your master's letter to the doctor?"

"Certainly I did."

"That is curious; for I happen to have here a letter which I found on the floor of the room we occupied at the tavern, and which I strongly suspect is the letter you were intrusted with. Will you see for yourself, sir, whether this is your letter or not?" said the man, handing to Ts'êng an unopened envelope, which he produced from his sleeve.

With a trembling hand Ts'êng took the letter, and at a glance recognised it as the one he had written with such eager haste, and with such a longing hope. The thought that but for the treachery of the wretch before him his little Primrose might have been still with him was more than he could bear. For a moment he fell back in his chair with quivering lips and cheeks as pale as death, and then as suddenly the blood rushed headlong through his veins, and with wild eyes and uttering savage curses he sprang from his chair and rushed upon Tan, who, accepting the turn things had taken, had fallen on his knees, and was performing the *kotow* with every token of humble submission.

With wild fury Ts'êng kicked at the bowing head of his follower, and might probably have been charged a second time with manslaughter, had not his guest dragged him by main force back to his chair and dismissed Tan from the room.

It was a long time before Ts'êng could recover his composure. His nerves were completely unstrung, and he trembled like a leaf. His friend, who was a determined fatalist, used every argument at his command to soothe his remorse and regrets. He pointed out that Heaven having doomed the death of little Primrose, nothing could have prevented it; that even if the doctor had come, he could not have lengthened out her life one moment beyond the time allowed her by the Fates; and that, therefore, though Tan's conduct had been infamous, it had not in any way influenced the result. "I quite admit that the man deserves punishment for his disobedience, and I would suggest that you should now order him to be bambooed on the spot. It will satisfy justice, and will, at the same time, be a relief to your feelings."

"It will certainly be a relief to me to see the fiendish brute suffer," said Ts'êng, "and it shall be done at once." So saying, he directed three of his servants to seize Tan and to flog him in the court-yard. The men, who were evidently not unused to the kind of business, dragged the offender in and stretched him face downwards on the stones of the yard. One then sat on his shoulders, another on his ankles, while a third, being provided with half a split bamboo, prepared to inflict chastisement. At a signal from Ts'êng the concave side of the bamboo descended on the back of the thighs of the culprit with tremendous force and effect. The wretched man's frame quivered throughout, and as blow after blow fell he uttered cries for mercy, and bitter groans which would have appealed to the heart of any one whose feelings were not deadened by mental tortures. But Ts'êng, in his present unhinged frame of mind, had no mercy, and if a restraining hand had not been outstretched he would have allowed the wretched man to die under the lash. As it was, his friend interfered, and warned Ts'êng that the punishment was becoming excessive. To this remonstrance Ts'êng yielded, and the blows were stayed. But Tan, whose cries had gradually died away into silence, remained motionless, and unconscious of the mercy which had been extended to him. Seeing his condition, the servants carried him off to his bed, where, under the influence of restoratives, he was by degrees brought back to life. But it was many days before he was able to move; and even then his weakness was so great, and his nerves so shattered, that he had the air of a man recovering from a long illness. If, however, Ts'êng had hoped that the punishment would have produced penitence, he was much mistaken. At the best of times Tan's temper was not good. He was by nature morose and revengeful, and a certain want of courage in his composition disposed him towards deceit. With regaining strength he brooded more and more over the treatment he had received, and he vowed a fierce vow that for every blow that had been inflicted on him he would exact a tenfold vengeance.

Meanwhile the anxiety, grief, and excitement of the last few days had reduced Ts'êng to the verge of illness, and his general debility added a new cause of anxiety to poor Golden-lilies' already overburdened bosom. So serious was his condition, that she persuaded him to pay a visit to his brother at Su-chow, for the sake of the change of scene and air. The remedy was exactly what he required; and after a fortnight's absence, he wrote to say that he was so much better that he should follow his letter at the interval of a day.

By this time Tan was able to walk, and so soon as he was assured of the date of his master s return, he absented himself from the house for the rest of the day. Towards evening he returned, and though his mood was exultant, he was strictly reticent as to his

"WHAT IS THE WARRANT FOR?" – "MURDER!" – *Page 64.*

doings while abroad. His fellow-servants were too busy to be inquisitive; and as his enfeebled condition still prevented him from serving, he was left to himself.

The next day, towards evening, as Ts'êng's chair turned into the road in which his house stood, two police-runners, who had been sitting on a doorstep opposite, rose and crossed over to Ts'êng's gateway. At the familiar shout of the chair-coolies, *Tung-chia lai-lo* ("The master has come"), the big folding-doors were thrown open, and the bearers were on the point of crossing the threshold, when one of the policemen advanced, and producing a warrant, ordered the coolies to stop and Ts'êng to dismount. Instinctively Ts'êng obeyed, and was for the first moment or two so dazed that he hardly seemed to be aware what was going on. By degrees the dress of the policeman, with his red-tasselled official cap and long robe, helped him to realise the situation, and he gasped out, "What is the warrant for?" "Murder," answered the man, as he laid his hand on Ts'êng's arm. It was fortunate for Ts'êng that he did so, for without some support he would have fallen prone to the ground. As it was, it was as much as the two men could do to support his tottering steps for a few yards, and then his legs refused to move, and his head fell forward on his chest as he dropped off into a dead faint. Seeing the condition of their master, the coolies brought forward his sedan, and the policemen accepting their aid, put the inanimate form of their prisoner into the chair, and directed the coolies to carry it to the prison at the district magistrate's *yamun*. The distance was not great, and the coolies, anxious to save their master from additional shame, hurried fast through the streets. On arriving at the *yamun*, they entered the front gates, and were then directed by the policemen to turn off to the left through a door, the insignia of which, a painted tiger's head with huge staring eyes and widely opened jaws, marked it as the entrance to the prison. Passing through this they entered a narrow passage, at the end of which was a courtyard, where the coolies were ordered to put down their load. It had never been the fate of either of these two men to find themselves within a prison before; and the sights which met their eyes made them shudder to think what their master's feelings would be when he awoke to consciousness and found himself in such a place.

In the courtyard itself, groups of prisoners, bound with heavy chains, were huddled together, whose appearance was enough to carry horror and compassion to the minds of all but those case-hardened by habit. Their faces were thin and worn, and bore the cadaverous hue which is commonly begotten by want and foul air; while the listless expression of their eyes and the languid movements of their limbs furnished additional testimony to the state of weakness to which they had been reduced. The condition of their persons was filthy in the extreme. Skin-disease in every form was rife among them; and it was plain that a rich harvest was ripening for death within the walls of the jail. As the poor wretches crowded round the sedan-chair to see who could be the new arrival who came in such state, the coolies instinctively drew back; and if the head jailer had not made his appearance at the moment, and with a sweeping blow and a curse driven his charges backwards, the still insensible Ts'êng would have been left in his chair. Scarcely less repulsive than the prisoners was the jailer, but for different reasons. There were no signs of want or ill health about him, nor was he dirtier than Chinamen of his class generally are, but a harder and more malignant face than his it is impossible to imagine. And that these outward signs were but the reflection of the savage cruelty of his character, was proved by the look of abject terror with which the prisoners regarded him. In a voice thick and grating, he ordered two of his myrmidons to manacle Ts'êng, and then to carry him into one of the cells which formed the eastern and western sides of the courtyard. Even from the outside these places looked more like wild-beast dens than the dwellings of human beings. The roofs were low, and a double row of strong wooden palisades, reaching from the ground to the eaves, guarded them in front. Into one of these dungeons, over whose portal was inscribed, as if in bitter mockery, the motto, "The misery of to-day may be the happiness of to-morrow," Ts'êng was carried. The coolies, determined to see the last of their master, followed him in. As they reached the door they recoiled as though a blast of a charnel-house had rushed out against them. Never were human senses assailed by an atmosphere more laden with pestilence and death. After a moment's hesitation, however, they mustered up courage to enter, and waited just long enough to see their master laid on the raised wooden platform which extended along the side of the den. As they were not allowed to do anything for him, and as the turnkeys promised that he should be looked after, they escaped into the open air.

True to their word, and possibly in the hope of a reward, the turnkeys applied water to Ts'êng's face and head, and succeeded in reawakening life. At first he began to move restlessly and to moan piteously, and then opened his lack-lustre eyes. For a moment or two he saw nothing, but by degrees his power of conscious sight returned, and he looked wildly round the cell. His first impression was that he had passed into a land of eternal punishment, such as he had heard Buddhists speak of, and he shrieked aloud for mercy. The sight, however, of the policeman who had served the warrant on him, recalled to his recollection the circumstances of his arrest; and as his real condition dawned upon him, he sank back on the stage, overcome with horror and despair. How long he lay in this condition he knew not, but he was aroused from it by the entrance of the prisoners from the courtyard, who were being driven in for the night. Already the platform was full enough, but with these new arrivals the overcrowding became excessive; and as the weary wretches struggled with their little remaining strength for the places nearest to the grating, they jostled Ts'êng, and fought across him like wild beasts, adding a new horror to his misery. The atmosphere of the den became also even fouler than before; and what with the heat and stench, Ts'êng began to feel feverish and ill. His head ached fiercely, his skin burnt, and his mouth was dry and parched. In his agony he called aloud for water; and though at first his cries were disregarded, his importunity prevailed with a prisoner less callous than the rest, who filled a tin mug from a tub which stood in the middle of the cell. The act of moving the water caused a fetid stench to rise from the slimy surface of the reservoir; and so foul were the contents of the mug, that, though burning with fever, Ts'êng could scarcely make up his mind to taste them. But thirsty men will swallow anything; and at last he drained the cup to its dregs, and even returned it to his benefactor with grateful thanks.

All night long he tossed about, burning with fever and tortured by delirium. His restlessness earned for him the anathemas of his fellow-prisoners, who, having been long inured to the foul atmosphere of the den, slept in comparative quiet. As daylight dawned the figures about him mixed themselves up with his delirious dreams, which, however, could add nothing to the horrors actually presented to his eye. Shocking as had been the aspect of his fellow-prisoners in the courtyard the day before, it was nothing to be compared to the condition of many of those whom weakness had prevented from groping their way into the outer air. One group of these were huddled together at the end of the platform, whose emaciated bodies and look of fierce agony told only too plainly that they were starving. One of their number had already been released from his tortures by death; and the rats, more conscious of the fact than the jailers, were gnawing at the only fleshy parts of his skeleton-like form. A like fate was the only portal of escape left to those about him, and eagerly they desired to meet it. Ever and anon sleep relieved Ts'êng's eyes from the contemplation of these horrors, and then in his dreams, as though by a law of contraries, he wandered in the asphodel meadows of Elysium, surrounded by every object calculated to gratify the imagination and delight the senses. The transition from these visions to a perception of his actual surroundings was sharp and bitter. In moments of reason he sought for the means of escape from the terrors of his present cell. He knew enough of prisons to know that it was in the power of the turnkeys to mitigate the sufferings of their charges, and he knew that money was the key to open the door of their sympathies. He remembered that when arrested he had some ten or twelve ounces of silver in his pocket, and he made up his mind to try the effect of these on the turnkey when he should come to open the cell in the morning. At last that happy moment arrived. The man who had turned the key on him the night before now threw open the door, and Ts'êng, in company with most of his fellow-prisoners, crawled out into the fresher air of the courtyard. As the turnkey passed through the yard, Ts'êng accosted him, and in exchange for the contents of his purse, procured a breakfast which was the feast of an epicure compared to the fare dealt out to the common herd.

Meanwhile Golden-lilies' night had been scarcely more pleasantly spent than her husband's; and to her also had occurred the idea that it would be possible to buy with money the consideration of the jailers. While it was yet early, therefore, she collected all the available cash in the house, and set out in her sedan-chair for the prison. The head jailer received the announcement of her name with a cynical smile. He had expected that she would come, and knew well the object of her visit. Accustomed to such interviews, and to the readiest means of turning them to the best account, he at first assumed a hard and unrelaxing manner, and yielded only to Golden-lilies' entreaties when he had drained her resources. The upshot, however, of the visit was, that Ts'êng was summoned before the jailer, and was told that, in consideration of his being untried, he should be removed to another courtyard, "where," said the jailer, with something approaching a smile, "I hope you will be more comfortable than you probably were last night." In fulfilment of this concession, Ts'êng was led off to a neighbouring compound, which appeared almost clean and healthy in comparison with the one he had just left. The prisoners in it also were fewer in number, and though they were dirty and unshaven, they were evidently of a higher class than Ts'êng's late companions. They welcomed Ts'êng with some attempts at conversation, and performed various kindly offices for him, which, in his weak state of health, were more than he had either energy or strength to accomplish for himself. One man in particular, a stout, cheery-looking son of Ham, was very kind and attentive; and as the day wore on, and they began to know more about one another, and the offences with which they were severally charged, this man did much to lighten the cares of all, and of Ts'êng in particular, to whom he seemed to have taken a liking. Of Ts'êng's prospects—"as I suppose," he said, "you are willing to be liberal with your money,"—he professed to take a hopeful view; while he did not conceal the fact that his own career would in all probability be quickly cut short.

"Instigating a rebellion is not a crime that finds mercy, even though it might be justified, as in my case, by the tyranny of the local mandarins."

"But if you are without hope, how can you possibly be as cheerful as you are?" said Ts'êng.

"Because I am a philosopher," said Lung—for that was his name; "because I have drunk deep at the fountain which inspired Lao-tsze, Chwang-tsze, and others, and have learnt with them the true value of life and the art of living and dying."

"The men you speak of were heretics," replied Ts'êng, "and went so far as even to speak disrespectfully of our great master Confucius. Nothing but disappointment must follow on faith in such as those."

"You boast yourself in Confucius, do you?" rejoined Lung. "I thought you did when you first came in, by your look of misery. Now tell me, how does he help you in your present difficulty? Which is in the best mental case—you who trust in the stereotyped phrases of that old formalist, or I who follow the kindly lead of the Taoist philosophers? You look on the future life with terrified uncertainty; while I, regarding it in its true light, see in it but a continuance of existence in a new shape."

"These are all fallacies."

"Show me that they are."

"Did not Confucius say, in answer to Ke Lu's question about a future state, 'We do not know about life, and how, then, can we know about anything beyond the grave?' And if Confucius's intelligence stopped short with life, who can possibly hope to peer beyond it?"

"And are you really such a blind follower of the blind as that comes to? Has it never occurred to you to ask yourself whence you came and whither you are going? But I need not put the question to you, for if you had, you would never tremble so at the bare idea of stepping over the brink. To me, the knowledge that the executioner's sword will help me to return to the Great Mother of all things, from whence I came and to which, in common with all created things, I must return, is no unpleasing prospect. I have played my part on this stage. I have dreamed my earthly dream, with its fancies, its nightmares, and its moments of pleasurable excitement, and now I am ready and willing to pass into the loving arms of 'Abyss Mother.' Here we Taoists have the advantage over you Confucianists. You strut about, talking loudly over the relations between man and man, parents and children, and sovereigns and ministers—all good things in their way—but you forget or close your eyes to the fact that existence does not end with what we call death. You limit your system to the short space of man's life upon earth, while we, overleaping all bounds of time, claim our right to immortality, and step with assurance into the grave."

"That is all very plausible," said Ts'êng, "but you have no evidence that there is any continuance of existence after death. No one has ever returned to life to give us his experiences, and your creed on this point must of necessity, therefore, be merely an assumption."

"Nay, it is more than that. Do we not see all around us that nothing in creation is ever absolutely destroyed? It suffers ceaseless change, but always exists. Look at the wood on a fire: it ceases to be wood after the flames have consumed it, but it reappears as smoke and ashes. Look at the leaves which strew the ground in autumn: decay transforms their shapes, but they do but change into mould, which again enters into the life of plants and trees,—and so created things go on for ever."

"That is a kind of reasoning that I don't understand," replied Ts'êng. "If you can produce any positive evidence that there is a future existence, I will believe it; but I cannot accept a faith which is based on an analogy of burnt wood and decayed leaves. And so to tell me to take comfort in the contemplation of a future state of happiness, is like telling a hungry man to satisfy his appetite by thinking of a feast, or a man shivering with cold to feel warm by imagining a roaring fire."

"So this is what it comes to; that Confucius serves as a guide through life when a man ought to be able to guide himself, and deserts you just at the moment when, in the face of death, you want some staff to support you, and some hand to lead you. But here comes the jailer, looking more like a demon than ever; he must have bad news for one of us."

At this moment the jailer entered with the list of those whose names had been marked with the vermilion pencil of the emperor for immediate execution, and turning to Lung, he told him, without any unnecessary verbiage, that his time had come. The seal thus set to the fate of his acquaintance was a severe shock to poor Ts'êng. His tongue refused to speak, and he durst not look on the face of the condemned man. But Lung was quite unmoved.

"You see," he said, addressing Ts'êng, "my race is run, and I only hope that if ever you should be in a like position, you may be enabled to face the future with the same composure that I do, and to place as sure a faith in the loving tenderness of the Great Mother of us all, as that which now supports me."

Ts'êng was too much overcome to utter a word, but wrung his friend's hands, and with weeping eyes watched him led off to be questioned by the judge before being borne to the execution-ground.

This event cast a gloom over the prison for the rest of the day; and the approach of night, even though it entailed a retreat into the close and fetid atmosphere of the cell, was a relief to all. The next morning, immediately after breakfast, the jailer paid another visit to the courtyard and summoned Ts'êng to appear before the magistrate. The contrast between his last interview with his judge and the present occasion, covered Ts'êng with shame and remorse. As he entered the judgment-hall he scarcely ventured to lift his eyes to his former host, who was seated behind a large table covered with red cloth, attended by secretaries, interpreters, and turnkeys. He thought it just possible that when the magistrate recognised him he would pay him some consideration. But these hopes were rudely dispelled when two of the executioners, who stood at the foot of the dais, taking him by the arms, forced him on his knees. At the same moment, at a signal from the magistrate, one of the secretaries read out the accusation, in which he was charged with having murdered "a wandering pedlar, named Ting."

"Are you guilty of this charge, or not guilty?" asked the magistrate, in a cold, clear voice.

"Not guilty, your Excellency," said Ts'êng, vaguely hoping that his denial would be sufficient.

"Call the witnesses," said the magistrate; and to Ts'êng's horror, at a sign from the secretary, Tan stepped forward and fell on his knees.

"Now tell us what you know of this matter," said the magistrate.

Thus adjured, Tan told the whole story from beginning to end, and though he laid great stress on the pressure Ts'êng had put upon him to induce him to help to bury the body, he, on the whole, made his statement plainly and truthfully. Still Ts'êng thought it possible that, if no other evidence was produced, his word would be taken against his servant's,—at all events, the only answer that occurred to his confused mind was a flat denial.

"The whole story, your Excellency, is a lie from beginning to end," he said, "and is invented by this man out of spite, in consequence of my having had occasion to flog him for a gross falsehood and breach of trust." The confident manner in which Ts'êng made this uncompromising assertion, evidently produced a favourable effect on the magistrate, who, turning to Tan, asked—

"Have you any evidence of the truth of your story?"

"Well, your Excellency, I can show you where we buried the body, and where it is at this moment, if it has not been removed."

At these words Ts'êng, who felt the ground slipping from under him, trembled all over, and would have fallen forward had not a turnkey supported him on his knees. These signs of trepidation were not unmarked by the magistrate, who ordered two policemen to go with Tan to exhume the body, and directed Ts'êng in the meantime to stand on one side. So completely had his nerves now forsaken him, however, that to stand was impossible, and he was therefore allowed to sit huddled up against an angle in the wall at the side of the court. Here he suffered all the mental tortures to which weak and cowardly natures are susceptible. Shame, remorse, and anger all tortured him in turns, and dominating all was the abject terror which possessed him. The knowledge that he was completely in the power of others over whom he had not the slightest influence or control;

that he was alone without a single friend to whom to turn for advice or help; that he was guilty of the crime laid to his charge; and that death at the hand of the executioner would in all probability be his fate,—was an instrument which plagued him with such intensity, that it almost bereft him of reason. Rocking himself to and fro, and moaning piteously, he sat the very picture of misery. Other cases were called on and disposed of, but he heard not a word, and was only recalled to consciousness by being dragged once again into the courtyard, and put on his knees before the tribunal. He knew that this meant that Tan had returned, and he instinctively felt that the body of the murdered man was close beside him, but he durst not look round. Almost lifeless, he knelt waiting for the first words, which seemed as though they were never to be uttered. At last they came.

"*Huddled up against an angle in the wall.*"

"Have you brought the body?"

"We have, your Excellency," answered Tan, "and here it is; we put it into this coffin as it has been dead for some time; shall we open it?"

"Wait," said the magistrate, who was evidently anxious to avoid that operation if possible, and turning to Ts'êng, he asked, "Do you still deny your guilt?"

"No," replied Ts'êng, who had now lost all hope; "but I did not mean to kill him, it was an accident, indeed it was. Oh, have mercy on me," cried the wretched man, "and spare my life! Punish me in any way, but oh, let me live!"

"Your pitiable cries for mercy," said the magistrate, "only make your conduct worse. You had no compassion on the man you murdered and who now lies there in evidence against you, and I shall therefore have none on you. I sentence you——"

At this moment a sound of voices and a rush of persons were heard at the other end of the courtyard. The magistrate paused and looked up, prepared to inflict the bastinado on the intruders, but their appearance warned him that something unusual had happened. Golden-lilies led the van, and falling on her knees before the magistrate, cried—

"Spare him, spare him, your Excellency! it is all a mistake. Ting is not dead, but is here."

At the sound of Golden-lilies' voice, Ts'êng awoke from the trance into which he had fallen at the magistrate's rebuke, and turned his lack-lustre eyes upon his wife. Her eager look gave him confidence, and following the direction of her outstretched finger, he beheld the old pedlar on his knees. But he was still too dazed to grasp the situation. Meanwhile Golden-lilies' volubility was unchecked.

"Ask him, your Excellency, and he will tell you he is the man; that the ferryman told a wicked lie; and that far from having been killed, he has not suffered the slightest inconvenience from his fall."

"But your husband has confessed that he murdered him," said the magistrate.

"The ferryman told him he had, and he believed him; but it was not true," urged Golden-lilies; "and just when I thought that the darkest hour of my life had come, when all hope of seeing my husband again alive seemed vanishing, who should knock at our door but the pedlar himself. Without waiting to hear his explanation, I have brought him with me; and now do let my husband go."

"Not so fast," said the magistrate. "I must first satisfy myself that this is Ting, and then I must inquire who that dead man yonder is, or rather was. Call Tan."

At this invocation Tan took up his former position on his knees; but in the interval since his last appearance he had lost confidence, and the turn events had taken did not, he saw clearly, reflect so brightly on his prospects as they did on Ts'êng's. He felt that he was compromised, though he could not understand it all, and was not quite sure how the magistrate would, on review, regard his conduct.

"Do you recognise that man?" asked the magistrate, pointing at Ting.

"Yes, your Excellency; he is Ting the pedlar, or his ghost."

"But in your evidence you charged your master with murdering Ting, and you swore that you buried him; and in support of your assertions you produce a body which is not Ting's, since Ting is here. How do you explain this?"

"All I can say, your Excellency, is, that my master ordered me to bury Ting; and Lai, the ferryman, told me that the man I buried was Ting."

"Arrest Lai and bring him before me at once," said the magistrate to a police-runner; "and meanwhile I will hear the pedlar's evidence. Bring him forward. Who are you?"

"My contemptible surname, your Excellency, is Ting, and my personal name is 'Heavenly Brightness.'"

"Tell me what you know of this matter."

"After leaving the house of his honour Ts'êng," said Ting, "I got into Lai's ferry-boat to cross the lake. On the way over I told him the story of the fracas at his honour's door, and showed him the silk which had been given me. He took a fancy to the pattern on it, and bought it from me, as well as the basket in which I carried it. Nothing else happened until just as we got to the other shore, when we saw the corpse of a man floating in the water. As I walked away from the shore I turned round and saw Lai rowing towards the body. I reached home the same evening and remained there until to-day, when I called at his honour's house. On showing myself at the door I was, to my surprise, hurried off here, and now I kneel in your Excellency's presence."

At this juncture Lai entered. The last few weeks' dissipation had not improved his appearance, and his ill-concealed terror at his present predicament added a ghastly paleness to his bleared and sallow complexion.

"How is this," said the magistrate, "that you have charged an innocent man with murder, and have palmed off on him the body of some one else as that of the man you said he had murdered?"

Seeing that circumstances were against him, Lai was silent.

"Now listen," said the magistrate: "you, Lai, are the principal culprit in this affair. You brought an unjust accusation against an innocent man, and by means of it extorted money from him. For these crimes I sentence you to receive a hundred blows with the large bamboo, and to be transported into Mongolia for five years. Because you, Tan, having connived at the concealment of what you believed to be a murder, charged your master with the murder out of a spirit of revenge, I sentence you to receive fifty blows on the mouth, and fifty blows with the large bamboo. And as to you, Ts'êng, though your conduct has been bad in attempting to conceal what you believed to be your crime, and in bribing others to silence, yet, in consideration of your imprisonment and of what you have gone through, I acquit you."

Never were more life-giving words uttered than those addressed by the magistrate to Ts'êng. Their effect was visible upon him physically; he seemed to grow in bulk under their gracious influence, and his face reverted from the pallor of death to the colour of life.

"May your Excellency live for ever," said he, as he *kotowed* before his judge, who, however, had left the judgment-seat before he had completed his nine prostrations. As the magistrate turned away from the hall, he met Mr Tso, who had come to call upon him.

"So our friend Ts'êng has got off, I see," said his visitor.

"Yes," said the magistrate, "but I have quite come round to your estimate of his character. He is a poor creature. I sent a much finer fellow to the execution-ground yesterday."

"Marked it as the entrance to the prison."—Page 65

THE TWINS.

FROM THE CHINESE OF WU MING.

THE saying commonly attributed to Mencius, that "Marriages are made in heaven," is one of those maxims which unfortunately find their chief support in the host of exceptions which exist to the truth which they lay down. Not to go further for an instance than the Street of Longevity, in our notable town of King-chow, there is the case of Mr and Mrs Ma, whose open and declared animosity to each other would certainly suggest that the mystic invisible red cords with which Fate in their infancy bound their ankles together, were twined in another and far less genial locality than Mencius dreamed of.

With the exception of success in money-making, fortune has undoubtedly withheld its choicest gifts from this quarrelsome couple. The go-between who arranged their marriage spoke smooth things to Ma of his future wife, and described her as being as amiable as she was beautiful, or, to use her own words, "as pliant as a willow, and as beautiful as a gem;" while to the lady she upheld Ma as a paragon of learning, and as a possessor of all the virtues. Here, then, there seemed to be the making of a very pretty couple; but their neighbours, as I have been often told, were not long in finding out that harmony was a rare visitant in the household. The daily wear and tear of life soon made it manifest that there was as little of the willow as of the gem about Mrs Ma, whose coarse features, imperious temper, and nagging tongue made her anything but an agreeable companion; while a hasty and irascible temper made Ma the constant provoker as well as the victim of her ill-humours.

By a freak of destiny the softening influences of the presence of a son has been denied them; but *en revanche* they have been blessed with a pair of the most lovely twin daughters, who, like pearls in an oyster-shell, or jewels in the heads of toads, have grown up amid their sordid surroundings free from every contamination of evil. They are beyond question the most beautiful girls I have ever seen. In figure they are both tall and finely shaped, with plastic waists and gracefully bending forms. In feature—for both Daffodil and Convolvulus, as they are called, are so exactly alike, that in describing one

I describe both—they are lovely, having eyebrows like half-moons, eyes which are so lustrous that one would expect them to shine in darkness, lips of the most perfect vermilion, finely shaped noses, and softly modelled cheeks. In fact, they are more like children of the gods than the daughters of men; and from all I have ever heard of them, their tempers and dispositions are counterparts of their outward appearance. All these charms of mind and of person were, however, quite lost upon their sordid mother, who until lately regarded them as though they were of the same mould as herself. So much so, that when they reached the prescribed marriageable age, instead of proposing to seek the empire for two incomparables to pair with such matchless beauties, she announced to her husband, in her usual brusque and overbearing manner, that she intended to look out for two rich young shopkeepers as husbands for "the girls." The moment she chose for making this announcement was not happily timed. She had already succeeded in ruffling Ma once or twice in the earlier part of the day, so that when she now blurted out her intention his colour rose with more than usual rapidity in his commonly sallow cheeks, and he replied angrily—

"I forbid your doing anything of the kind. You have no business to meddle with matters which don't pertain to you. Your duty in life is to obey me, and to do nothing without my instructions."

"Hai-yah! If I did that," said Mrs Ma, now thoroughly aroused, "the household would soon come to a pretty pass. What do you know about managing matters? You remind me of the owl which made itself look like a fool by trying to sing like a nightingale!"

"You ignorant woman!" replied her husband; "how dare you bandy words with me! Don't you know that Confucius has laid it down as an imperishable law that a woman before her marriage should obey her father, and after her marriage her husband?"

"And do you know so little of the Book of Rites," said Mrs Ma, nothing abashed, "as not to be aware that the mother should arrange the marriages of her daughters? So just you leave this matter to me. If you want to be doing something, open your chemist's shop again. What will it matter if you do poison a few more people by dispensing the wrong drugs?"

"You infamous creature! how dare you utter such slanders! If you ever again venture on such unparalleled insolence, I will divorce you! for remember that one of the seven grounds for divorce is violence of language. And how would you like to be turned adrift into the cold world at your age, and with your anything but pleasing appearance?"

This last shot told, and Mrs Ma flung herself out of the room without a word, contenting herself with expressing her anger and defiance by banging the door furiously after her. No sooner was the door shut than Ma took paper and pencil and wrote to invite his friend Ting "to direct his jewelled chariot to the mean abode of the writer, who was preparing a paltry repast for his entertainment." Ting was one of Ma's oldest friends, and, being linked to a wife of a harridanish temperament, had a common bond of union with him. Like Ma also, he was secretly afraid of his better half, and his counsel, therefore, on the several occasions of domestic dispute on which he had been consulted, had naturally tended rather towards artifice than open war. Ma's note at once suggested to Ting a family disagreement, and he lost no time in obeying the summons, being always glad to find fresh evidences that others were as evilly circumstanced as himself. He was a tall, stout man, with a loud voice, but wanting that steadiness of eye which should match those outward seemings. By many people he was credited with a firm and somewhat overbearing character; but his wife probably showed more discernment when on one occasion, after a shrill outburst, she reminded him that "an empty pot makes the greatest noise."

As Ting entered Ma's room the two friends greeted one another cordially, and into the sympathetic ear of his guest Ma poured the story of his griefs.

"And now, what do you advise me to do?" asked the host. "My insignificant daughters have arrived at a marriageable age, and though they profess an aversion to matrimony and a contempt for the young men of this place, I consider it my duty to settle them in life. But I see clearly that if I am to do it at all, I alone must be the doer. My wife's views are so invariably opposed to mine, that it is hopeless to attempt to act in harmony with her."

"Well," replied Ting, "I myself always act on the principle of the proverb, 'What the eye does not see, the heart does not grieve after.' I have on several occasions made family arrangements without letting my wife into the secret until the time for interference has passed, and then, of course, she has been compelled to accept the inevitable. It is true the artifice has resulted in very unpleasant outbursts of wrath; but that is nothing—nothing, my dear Ma." Here Ting's voice, in spite of his brave words, trembled, as a recollection of certain domestic scenes came back to his memory. "Besides, I have in this way succeeded in asserting my position as master of my own household. And my advice to you in your present circumstances is that you should do likewise. If you have made up your mind to marry your daughters, employ a go-between to look out fitting partners, and make the necessary arrangements without saying anything to your wife about it. Then, when the presents have been sent and the cards exchanged, she will find it as easy to dam up the river with her pocket-handkerchief as to bar their marriages."

"Excellent! excellent!" said Ma; "I will act upon your advice. But I must be very circumspect, Ting, very circumspect; for Mrs Ma has a number of old cronies about her, who gather gossip from stone walls, rumours from the wind, and scandal from everything."

"Perhaps then it would be as well," replied Ting, rising to take his leave, "if you were to make use of my study for seeing the go-between and others whom you may wish to employ in the affair. It is quite at your disposal."

"Ten thousand thanks," said Ma. "Your advice

has made a man of me, Ting, and your kindness has carved for itself a place in my heart in which it will be for ever enshrined."

Meanwhile Mrs Ma, although for the moment discomfited, was by no means inclined to give up the struggle. After a short communing with herself she sent for Daffodil and Convolvulus, and announced to them her intention of forthwith providing them with husbands of their own rank in life, directing them at

"*But, mother, we do not wish to marry.*"

the same time to preserve absolute silence on the subject to all but old "Golden-lilies," their maid and chaperon.

"But, mother, we do not wish to marry," said Convolvulus; "least of all to be tied for life to the sort of young man whom you are kind enough to contemplate for us. Why should we not remain as we are?"

"You are too young to understand such matters," replied Mrs Ma. "I have seen mischief enough arise from leaving young girls unmarried, and I am determined that you shall not be exposed to any such danger. Besides, I have been so bothered lately by suitors, who, it seems, have heard of your beauty, that I shall have no peace until you are settled."

"Remember, mother," put in Daffodil, "that as you have no sons, you and father are dependent on us to tend and wait upon you. Then, mother, we are so perfectly happy in each other's society that we need no other companionship, and it would break our hearts to be separated from each other and from you."

"I am touched by your expressions of affection, my children," answered their mother; "but my mind is quite made up, as I have just told your father, who is foolish enough to think, poor man, that he ought to have the management of the business. And now go back to your embroideries, and remember what I have said to you about keeping the matter secret."

Mrs Ma's announcement, although not altogether unexpected, fell with a heavy blow upon the twins, who had other and deeper reasons than those they had expressed for disliking the idea of having husbands of their mother's choice forced upon them. Women seldom, if ever, in the first instance give their real reasons, at least in China. Their habit is to fence them round with a succession of outworks, in the shape of plausible excuses, which, if strong enough to resist the questioner, preserve inviolate their secret motives. If, however, they are driven by persistence out of the first line of defence, they retreat to the second, and so on, until the citadel is reached, when they are commonly obliged to yield, though even then they generally manage to march out with all the honours of war. In this case Mrs Ma had no motive for breaking the fence of the twins, and so never learnt, as she might otherwise have possibly done, that though the garden wall was high, it was not too hard to climb, and that often when she fancied her daughters were engaged at their embroideries, or practising their guitars, they were flirting merrily in the garden with the two young scholars, under the chaperonage of "Golden-lilies," to whom recollection brought a fellow-feeling for such escapades, and who always carefully watched over her charges, though at a judicious distance. These two youths, Messrs Tsin and Te, presented the real obstacles to the adoption of Mrs Ma's proposals by the twins. And it was at least evidence of the good taste of the young ladies that they preferred them to the young men of the shopkeeper class, among whom their mother thought to find them husbands. It was true that neither Tsin nor Te had at that time much of this world's goods, nor did there appear any immediate prospect of their being able to marry; for their fathers, who were ex-officials, were unendowed with anything beyond the savings they had accumulated during their terms of office, and these were not more than enough to enable them to end their days in retired comfort.

In these circumstances the ambitions of the young men centred in their chance of winning official rank at the examinations. Of Tsin's success no one who had sounded the depth of his scholarship had any doubt. Te, however, was by no means so gifted. His essays were dull reading, and his odes were wooden things, painfully elaborated in accordance with purely mechanical rules. He had none of the facility with which Tsin struck off a copy of verses, and could no more have penned the lines to Daffodil's eyebrows, which first attracted the attention of the sisters to the young scholars, than he could have flown. It was on the occasion of the Feast of Lanterns at the beginning of this year, that Tsin and Te first became aware of the existence of the twins, who, under the charge of Golden-lilies, were on the evening of that festival admiring the illuminations in the streets. Struck by the incomparable beauty of the young ladies, the youths followed them about in blank amazement, until Tsin's imagination having been suddenly fired by seeing an expression of delight pass over Daffodil's beaming countenance at the sight of an illumination more brilliant than usual, he hurriedly penned a stanza, in which the ideas of willow-leaf eyebrows and jade-like features were so skilfully handled, that when it fell into that young lady's hands she was lost in admiration at the grace and beauty of the lines. A hurried glance of acknowledgment was enough to keep the young men at the heels of the twins until the portals of the ex-chemist closed upon them; and when, on the next afternoon, Convolvulus found in the summer-house a stanza marked by all the grace of diction which characterised the ode of the previous day, she had no hesitation in ascribing the authorship to the same gifted being. This message of homage was a prelude to a hurried visit paid and received beneath the bunches of wistaria which hung around the favourite garden retreat of the twins, and this again to other and longer interviews, in which Tsin gradually came to devote himself to Daffodil, and Te to Convolvulus.

It was while toying at one such meeting that the twins were summoned to hear the designs which their mother had formed for their future; and when they left the maternal presence, it was with feelings akin to despair that they poured their griefs into Golden-lilies' sympathetic bosom. "What are we to do?" was their plaintive cry.

"Do?" said Golden-lilies cheerily—"why, do as the juggler did who was sentenced to death last year."

"You have always some wise saying or queer story ready; dear Golden-lilies. But explain; what did the juggler do except die?"

"That is just what he did not do, for when the Emperor told him that his life should be spared on condition that he made the Emperor's favourite mule speak, the man undertook to do it within twelve months by the calendar."

"What a fool he must have been!"

"So his friends said; but he replied, 'Not so, for many things may happen in a year: the mule may die, or the Emperor may die, or I may die; and even if the worst comes to the worst, and none of these things happen, I shall at least have had another year of life.' Now, though you are not in such a parlous state as the juggler was, yet, as you cannot resist your mother, you had better appear to submit, and trust to the chapter of accidents."

But Mrs Ma was evidently disposed to leave as little as possible to accident, for the very next morning she sallied out in her sedan-chair, and paid a visit to a well-known "go-between" in the town. This woman, delighted to have the credit of arranging the marriage of the beautiful twins, chose from her list of bachelors two young men, one the son of a silk-mercer and the other of a salt-merchant, who fulfilled Mrs Ma's main requirement of being rich.

"They are nice young men, too," she added, "though neither of them is likely to attract the admiration of the goddess of the North Star like the matchless Chang-le. But if ugly men never mated, the imperial race of China would soon die out."

"I don't care a melon-seed," said Mrs Ma, as she ate two or three of those delicacies from the dainty dish by her side, "about beauty in a man. None can be called deformed but the poor: money is beauty, and to my mind the true deformity is an empty purse. So please make the proper overtures at once, and let me know the result. I have reasons for wishing to preserve secrecy in this matter, and I would therefore beg you not to talk of it until all is arranged."

It was not long before the go-between reported confidentially that her proposal had been received both by the silk-mercer Yang and the salt-merchant Le on behalf of their sons with enthusiasm. Nor did the fortune-teller throw any obstacles in the way of the speedy fulfilment of Mrs Ma's schemes; for the almanac pointed with unmistakable clearness to the next full moon as being one of the most fortunate in the whole year for marriages.

Everything seemed therefore to lie level with the wish of Mrs Ma; and under the combined influences of good fortune and satisfaction evoked from the conviction that she was doing her duty as a mother, her good-nature knew no bounds. She was even civil to Ma, and in her superior way smiled to herself at the beaming self-content which had lately come over him, and which she naturally regarded as a reflection of her own good-humour. As the day for receiving the presents approached, she chuckled to see how easily he was persuaded to have the chairs and divan in the reception-hall re-covered and the walls redecorated. On the day itself—poor foolish man!—far from expressing any surprise at the superlative toilet in which she had bedecked herself, he paid her the compliment of likening her to a fairy from the palace of the "Royal Mother of the West," and even went the length, as though following her example, of arraying himself in his costliest garments. As the day advanced, the actions of each seemed to have a strange fascination for the other; and when, at the usual evening hour for the presentation of betrothal presents, the merry strains of the "Dragon and the Phœnix," played by more than one band, struck upon their ears, they glanced at one another with gratified curiosity rather than surprise. As the noise in the street swelled into a roar compounded of

"THE MERRY STRAINS OF THE 'DRAGON AND THE PHOENIX' PLAYED BY MORE THAN ONE BAND."

bands, drums, and the shouts of coolies, Mrs Ma's pride rose at the thought that she had succeeded in capturing such liberal and munificent suitors, and she had almost forgotten the opposition of her husband when four young men, bearing letters, and each leading a goose and a gander—the recognised emblems of conjugal affection—followed by servants carrying a succession of rich presents, advanced to the audience hall. That her two *protégés* should have sent eight geese appeared to her unnecessary, although she accepted the multiplication of the birds as a pretty token of the ardour of the lovers; but her sense of this excess was soon lost in her admiration of the unusually numerous gifts which now filled the courtyard.

With many deep reverences the young men presented their letters to Ma, who was at first too much dazed by the confusion which reigned about him to do more than to incline his head and open the envelopes. As he read the first letter, however, his confused expression of countenance was exchanged for one of puzzled surprise.

"There is," he said, "some mistake here. I know nothing of this Mr Yang who writes. You must," he added, turning to the young man who had presented the letter, "have come to the wrong house by mistake."

"Pardon me," replied the young gentleman, "your humble servitor has made no mistake, unless, indeed, you are not the honourable father of the incomparable twins whom you have deigned to betroth to my principal, Mr Yang, and his friend, Mr Le."

The mention of these names recalled Mrs Ma to the actualities of the position; and, advancing towards her husband, she said with some embarrassment—

"There is no mistake in the matter. I told you that I should arrange our daughters' marriages, and I have done so. Messrs Yang and Le are the gentlemen I have chosen, and these are their presents in due form."

For a moment Ma looked at her in angry astonishment, and then, as the whole affair took shape in his mind, he lost all control over himself, and, trembling with passion, he broke out—

"You stupid, obstinate woman, how dare you disobey my orders and practise this deceit upon me? By what pretence of right have you ventured to interfere in this matter? You have brought disgrace upon me and infamy upon yourself. *I* have arranged alliances for the twins with the sons of my friends Messrs Tsai and Fung, and it is these they shall marry and no others!" Then turning to Yang's and Le's young squires, he added with scant courtesy—"Take away your gifts, young men, and tell your principals that this rebuff serves them right for dealing in an underhand way with a headstrong woman."

"Don't listen to him," cried Mrs Ma. "I accept your presents."

"Take them away!" shouted Ma.

"You shameless boor!" screamed Mrs Ma—"you miserable, vapouring, good-for-nothing! Do you talk to me of 'daring' and 'venturing'? Why, you may thank Buddha that you have got a wife who knows how and when to act; and I tell you that your friends Tsai and Fung may as well try to join the hare in the moon as hope to raise the veils of my daughters. So if these young men represent them they had better be off at once and take their rubbish with them."

This was more than Ma's irascible nature was able to endure, and raising his hand to strike, he rushed

"Mrs Ma stood ready for the assault."

at his wife. Fortunately his servants were near enough to intervene, and an exchange of blows—for Mrs Ma had seized a flute from an amazed musician, and stood ready for the assault—was for the moment averted. Foiled in finding the natural outlet for his rage, Ma, with as wild gesticulations as were possible with a man holding each arm and a third dragging at his skirts, shouted orders to his servants to turn

Yang's and Le's squires, with their presents, out into the street. With equal vehemence Mrs Ma invoked the direst misfortunes and deepest curses on the head of any one who ventured to lay hands on them, and at the same time called on her partisans to throw the other people and their gifts out of doors. The hubbub thus created was aggravated by the incursion of idlers from the street, some of whom presently took sides, as the squires and their followers showed signs of acting on the taunts and adjurations of Ma and his wife. From words the adverse hosts speedily came to blows, and a scene of indescribable confusion ensued. The presents, which had made such a goodly show but a few minutes before, were broken to pieces and scattered over the courtyard; while the eight geese, with outstretched wings and wild cacklings, flew, seeking places of refuge. With impartial wisdom the servants of the house, aided by some unbiassed onlookers, threw their weight on the combatants in the direction of the door. By this manœuvre the courtyard was gradually cleared, and eventually the front gates were closed on the surging, fighting crowd, which was dispersed only when some few of the ringleaders had been carried off to the magistrate's *yamun.*

As a neighbour and an acquaintance of Ma, I thought it best, on being informed of what had taken place, to call in to see if I could be of any use. I had some difficulty in getting inside the front gates; but when I did, a scene of confusion presented itself such as I have never seen equalled. The courtyard was covered with *débris,* as though some typhoon had been creating havoc in an upholsterer's shop; while in the audience-hall Ma was inflicting chastisement on his wife with a mulberry-twig, which he had evidently torn from the tree at hand in the yard. I was fortunately in time to prevent the punishment becoming severe, though at the time I could not but feel that Mrs Ma's conduct was of a kind which could only be adequately punished by corporal chastisement.

As a husband and a Confucianist, I deprecate the use of the rod towards a wife except in extreme cases. There are, however, some women whose intellects are so small and their obstinacy so great that reasoning is thrown away upon them. They have nothing to which one can appeal by argument; and with such persons bodily fear is the only fulcrum on which it is possible to rest a lever to move them. From all I hear, Mrs Ma is a typical specimen of this class. She prides herself on her obstinacy, which she regards as a token of a strong mind, and she is utterly destitute of that intelligence which should make her aware of the misery and discomfort it causes to those about her. No camel is more obstinate and no donkey more stupid than she.

But while quite recognising this, I could not but feel some compassion for her, as, weeping and dishevelled, she escaped from the hall when I succeeded in releasing her from her husband's wrath. At first Ma's fury was so uncontrollable that I could do nothing with him; but gradually he quieted down, and, acting on my advice, went over to his friend Ting to consult as to what should be done in the very unpleasant circumstances in which he was placed. It was plain that some decided step would have to be taken, as the arrest of some of the rioters had brought the whole affair within the cognisance of the mandarins, and it is always best in such matters to be the one to throw the first stone. After much discussion it was, as I afterwards learned, decided that Ma should present a petition to the prefect, praying him, in the interest of marital authority and social order, to command the fulfilment of the contract entered into by the petitioner with Fung and Tsai.

On the following morning Ma, in pursuance of this arrangement, presented himself at the prefect's *yamun*, and, after having paid handsome *douceurs* to the doorkeeper and secretary, was admitted into the august presence of his Excellency Lo. Having only lately arrived in the prefecture, Lo's appearance had been hitherto unknown to Ma, who was much awed and impressed by the dignified airs and grand ways of his Excellency. A man severe he is and stern to view, and yet beneath his outward seeming there is a strong undercurrent of human nature, held in check, it is true, by the paralysing effect of our educational system, but still capable of being aroused and worked upon at times. As Ma knelt before him he glanced down the memorial, and demanded a full explanation of the circumstances. Nothing loath, Ma poured forth his version of the story, in which he by no means extenuated his wife's conduct, and wound up by emphasising the importance of checking the insubordination of the women, which was becoming only too prevalent in that neighbourhood.

"You certainly have made out a *primâ facie* case

for further investigation," said the prefect; "and what you say about women is, to your credit, precisely in accord with the teachings of Confucius, who laid down that 'women should yield absolute obedience to their husbands, and that beyond the threshold of their apartments they should not be known either for good or for evil.' I shall therefore summon your wife to appear at once before me; and meanwhile you may stand aside."

The summoning officer was not long in executing his mission, and the time had scarcely begun to hang heavily on Ma's hands when Mrs Ma entered the *yamun*. That lady looked anything but comfortable when she saw her husband talking with an assured air to the officers of the court, and answered his glance of recognition with the kind of look that a house-dog gives a stranger cur when it crosses his threshold. On learning that Mrs Ma had arrived, the prefect at once took his place on the bench; and as both disputants fell on their knees in the courtyard, he ordered Mrs Ma to explain her conduct in disobeying the commands of her husband.

"May it please your Excellency," she began, "I am a poor ignorant woman."

"So far I am with you," said the prefect; "but go on with your story."

"And, your Excellency, I have always tried to do my duty by my husband and children."

"That is not the point. Tell me why, when your husband had forbidden you to interfere in the matter of the marriage of your daughters, you persisted in doing so."

"May it please your Excellency, my great-grandmother——"

"Oh, may curses rest on your great-grandmother!" shouted the prefect, losing patience. "Speak to the matter in hand or you shall be flogged."

"I was only going to explain, your Excellency."

"Now take care what you are saying."

"It is true my husband told me that he would arrange our daughters' marriages, but I knew that anything he touched he marred, and I thought, therefore, that as I had always been told, at least by my great——" A warning glance from the prefect here checked her eloquence, and she went on—"I have always learned that the marriage of a daughter is the particular province of her mother. I should never have dreamed, your Excellency, of interfering if it had been our son's marriage. Not that we have a son, your Excellency, though many is the time I have been to the temple of Kwanyin to pray for one; and as to money, your Excellency——"

"Bring a one-inch bamboo," said the prefect to one of the lictors.

"Oh, please spare me, your Excellency, and I will say anything you wish!"

"All I want is that you should tell the truth and speak only the record. Do this, and I will listen; lie or wander, and I shall flog you."

"Well then, your Excellency, I found also that the two young men selected by my husband were in no way proper matches for my daughters, who are very beautiful. One of these wretched youths is blind in one eye, and the other has one leg shorter than its fellow. In these circumstances I took the matter in hand, and discovered two veritable dragons, who were yearning to link their fate with the pair of phœnixes who rest beneath my humble roof. As destiny decreed, my husband's cripples sent their betrothal presents at the same moment that Messrs Yang and Le sent theirs. Upon this my husband gave way to wild fury, broke the presents to atoms, beat the servants, and flogged your humble servant until she was one mass of bruises."

"Is it true that these *protégés* of yours are as your wife describes them?" asked the prefect of Ma.

"No, your Excellency; she has grossly exaggerated their defects. It is true that the sight of one of Fung's eyes is partially affected, and that Tsai's legs are not quite of an equal length, but the difference between them is so slight that it is outwardly invisible, and is only perceptible if he walks over a wooden floor, when there is a slightly hop-and-go-one sound about his steps. But, your Excellency, she would have been wise to have remembered the proverb, 'Don't laugh at your neighbour's wart when your own throat is disfigured by a wen;' for it is as well known as that your Excellency is the quintessence of wisdom, that Yang is only, as we people say, nine parts of a whole; and as for young Le, he bears so evil a reputation that no respectable citizen will allow him to enter his doors."

"Well, if this were a matter which only concerned you two, I should not trouble myself further about it, for you are a pair of the simplest of simpletons; but as your daughters' interests are at stake, I have thought it right to send for them, that I may find out what they feel on the subject."

At this moment the twins entered the court, and advanced with graceful modesty, swaying from side to side like tender shrubs gently moved by a passing breeze. Never had they looked more lovely; their jade-like complexions, exquisite features, and lustrous eyes lent so ethereal a beauty to their budding womanhood that they seemed more than mortal. With the winsomest mien, and wielding their fans as only Chinese women can, they bowed low before the prefect, and then stood awaiting his orders. The poor man gazed on them as a man gazes on spirits from the other world. He had looked up as they entered, expecting to see in them repetitions of their vulgar-looking parents; but to his unutterable surprise they stood before him resplendent as the moon on the fourteenth night, and as fascinating as fairies. As it happened, they had just arrayed themselves in their most becoming costumes in expectation of a visit from Tsin and Te, when the prefect's summons came. Every charm, therefore, which personal adornment could add to their natural beauty was present with them, and the picture they made as they stood in the middle of the courtyard was one which struck the spectators dumb with astonishment. The prefect dropped his pencil, and seemed quite to forget that anything was expected of him; and for the moment no one, except the twins and their parents, did expect anything from him; for one and all—secretaries, *ting-chais*, lictors, and clerks —were so ravished by the sight, that all consciousness of the fitness of things was lost to view. After some moments of silence, which seemed to the twins like so many hours, the prefect awoke from his rapt astonishment, and said—

"Are you really the daughters of these people before me? Is it possible that nature should have played such a trick, and should have moulded you in manners as in shape, in blood and in virtue, on a model as widely separated from your parents as earth is from heaven?"

"May it please your Excellency," replied Daffodil, in a low and nervous tone, "we are the children—the only children—of these our parents."

"Come nearer," rejoined the prefect, in a voice that had no stern judicial ring about it, "and speak without reserve to me; for if I do not espouse your cause and shield you from wrong, may my father's ashes be scattered to the wind, and my mother's grave be dishonoured. Tell me, now, have you any desire to marry any of the four suitors your father and mother have provided for you? and if you have, tell me to which you incline."

"We know nothing of these young men, your Excellency," said Daffodil.

"Well, when you hear that, according to your parents' description, one is blind, another lame, a third silly, and the fourth wicked, I should hardly expect that you would care to make their acquaintance. However, as they are in attendance I shall have them in, that you may see what manner of men they are." Turning to an officer, he added, "Send in the four suitors in this case."

As the young men entered, all eyes were turned towards them, and certainly a sorrier quartet it would be difficult to find anywhere. Their natural failings fully justified the description given of them by Ma and his wife, and were in this instance exaggerated by the consciousness of the ordeal they were called upon to undergo. The prefect looked at them with surprise and disgust; and the twins, who held Tsin and Te as their models, regarded them with horror from behind their fans.

"A sorrier quartet it would be difficult to find."

"Well?" said the prefect, turning to Daffodil and Convolvulus.

"Oh, your Excellency!" plaintively ejaculated the twins in one breath.

"I quite understand you, and your verdict is exactly what I should have expected; and since it is plain to me,—come a little nearer; I fear you cannot hear what I say,—that your parents are as incapable of understanding your value as monkeys are of appraising the price of apple-green jade, I shall take on myself the matter of your marriages. Are not prefects 'the fathers and mothers of the people'? and if so, then I am both your father and your mother. Put yourselves into my hands, then. Trust in me; and if I do not do the best I can for you, may I die childless, and may beggars worship at my tomb!"

"How can we thank you," said Daffodil, who was always readiest with her words, "for your boundless condescension and infinite kindness towards your handmaidens? May your Excellency live for ten thousand years, and may descendants of countless generations cheer your old age!"

"Thank you for your good wishes," said the prefect. "I must take time to consider the course I shall pursue, and will let you know the result." Then turning to Ma and his wife, he said in quite another tone—"Take your daughters home, and do not venture to make any arrangements for their future until you hear from me."

So saying he rose, but, contrary to his usual habit, waited to arrange his papers until the sylph-like forms of the twins had disappeared through the folding-doors, when he retired precipitately.

The next morning Ma was surprised by a visit from the prefect, who had found it necessary, he said, to inform the twins in person of his intentions towards them. Having greeted his wards with all the affection of a guardian, he said—

"On thinking over the matter of your marriages, I have determined to hold an examination preliminary to the coming official examination, and I propose to offer you as the prizes to be awarded to the two scholars who shall come out at the top of the list. In this way we shall have at least a guarantee that your husbands will be learned, and likely to gain distinction in official life."

"But suppose," put in Convolvulus timidly, "they should be married men?"

"Ah, I never thought of that!" said the prefect, laughing. "Well, I will tell you what I will do. It happens that a hunter brought me in this morning a brace of the most beautiful gazelles, and these I will give to the two top married men, as dim and bleared emblems of the still more lovely creatures which will fall to the lot of the two successful bachelors."

The prefect accompanied his remark with a smile and bow which added another tinge of colour to the blushes which had already suffused the brilliant cheeks of the twins, whose modest confusion had scarcely subsided when he took his departure.

The appearance, two or three days after this interview, of a semi-official proclamation announcing the examination and specifying the prizes in store for the winners, produced the wildest excitement in the town. The proceedings before the prefect had become notorious, and the rare beauty of the twins was, if possible, exaggerated by the thousand-tongued rumours which spread of their exceeding loveliness. To Daffodil the ordeal suggested no uneasiness. For, feeling confident of the surpassing talent of Tsin, she entertained no doubt that he would come out first upon the list. But with Convolvulus the case was different; for, though devotedly attached to Te, she had wit enough to recognise that his literary talents were not on a par with his distinguished appearance. The uneasiness she thus felt found vent in words at one of the stolen interviews in the arbour, and Te frankly admitted that he had been tortured by the same misgiving.

"If I could only dive into the prefect's mind," he said, "and find out what themes he has chosen for the two essays, I should have no fear."

These words sank deep into Convolvulus's soul, and in a conversation with Daffodil, in which she expressed her fears for Te, she repeated what he had said, adding—

"Do you think that we could worm out of the prefect something about the themes he is going to set?"

"I do not know, but we might try," replied her sympathetic sister. "The best plan would be, I think, that we should express in a casual way a liking for some classical piece, and it is possible that to pay us a compliment he might be kind enough to choose the themes out of it. For, dear old man, I saw from behind my fan a look in his eyes when he made us that pretty speech the other day that made me think of mother's saying, 'Men propose and women dispose.' Only yesterday dear Tsin taught me a lovely ode out of the 'Book of Poetry,' beginning—

> 'See where before you gleams the foaming tide
> Of Tsin and Wei down-sweeping in their pride.'

It was so pretty of him to choose an ode in which his own dear name occurs, was it not? Now, don't you think that in the letter we have to write to the prefect to-day about the copy of the proclamation he sent us, we might put in a quotation from this ode? It would at least please him, for I know he is fond of poetry, and it is possible that it might draw a remark from him which we may turn to account. It is full of lines which would make capital themes."

"Oh, Daffodil, how clever you are! If you and Tsin have sons they will all, I am sure, be *Chwang-yuen.*[1] Your device is excellent. Let us set to work at once to compose the letter."

So down they sat to the task, and after much cogitation, Daffodil drafted the following:—

"May it please your Excellency,—Your humble servants on their knees have received the jade-like epistle and proclamation which you deigned to send them. With rapture they have admired the pearl-like style of your brilliant pencil, and with endless gratitude they recognise your kindness and bounty, which are as wide and far-reaching as 'the gardens beyond the Wei' described in the 'Book of Poetry.'"

"Now, what do you think of that?" said Daffodil,

[1] The title of the senior wrangler of the empire.

as she put down her pencil. "*I* think it is neat. It brings in the reference to the ode without any seeming effort, and will, if I mistake not, tickle our friend's fancy for classical quotations."

"Oh, it is excellent," said Convolvulus. "With the twig so cleverly limed, I feel sure we shall catch our bird."

And the results proved Convolvulus to be right; for on the following day the prefect called again, and in conversation with the twins, with whom he had now grown familiar, he remarked—

"So I see you have read the 'Book of Poetry.'"

"Yes," said Convolvulus; "and it was such a pleasure to be able to quote our favourite ode in writing to our dearest friend."

The prefect, touched and pleased at this artless expression of regard, rejoined—

"It so happens that that is one of my favourite odes also. The description," added he, waxing enthusiastic, "of the wide-sweeping rivers, and the lovely gardens, with the admixture of human interests in the mention of lovers toying beneath the shade, presents to my mind a picture which is literally laden with beauty and delight."

"Though, of course, I am quite incapable of understanding *all* that you mean, it has occurred to me in reading the ode," replied Daffodil, "that every line is like a seed of corn, which, if properly treated, may be made to bring forth rich literary fruit."

"I cannot help thinking, Miss Daffodil," said the prefect, "that if you were to enter the lists at the examination you would probably win yourself."

"What a barren triumph it would be!" said Daffodil, laughing. "But if I competed at all," she added, "I should insist on your taking this ode as our text, and then I should reproduce the ideas you have just given us, and win the prize."

"Well, I tell you what I will do if you will keep my secret," said he. "I *will* give the themes from this ode, and then you and your sister will be able to judge whether the winners deserve the prizes. But what is the matter with your sister?"

This exclamation was caused by Convolvulus dropping her teacup on to the floor and breaking out into hysterical sobbing.

"Oh, she is rather subject to these attacks at this time of the year," said Daffodil, running to her side. "Will you excuse my attending to her?"

"Oh, don't think of me for a moment. Please look after your sister. I will go off at once, and shall send over in the afternoon to inquire how she is."

As the door closed on the prefect, Convolvulus sobbed out: "Oh, how stupid I have been! But I could not help it. Dear Te is now safe."

That afternoon there were great rejoicings in the summer-house, and Daffodil's *finesse* was eulogised in terms which to an unprejudiced observer might have seemed adulatory. And it was generally agreed between the four lovers that by steady application during the month which intervened before the examination, Te might easily make himself so completely master of all that had been written on the ode in question that he could not fail to succeed. With ready zeal, on the very next morning he set to work at the commentaries, and beginning with Mao's, he waded carefully through the writings of every weighty critic down to the present time. In the intervals of leisure he practised essay-writing under the guidance of Tsin, and made such progress that Convolvulus was in raptures; and even Daffodil, reflecting the opinion of Tsin, was loud in her praises of his diligence and success.

At last the examination day arrived, and armed with the good wishes and benedictions of the twins, the two friends betook themselves to the prefect's *yamun*. On entering the courtyard they found that rows of tables, separated by temporary partitions on the sides and at the back, were ranged in the usually empty space. At the door was a secretary—a stranger—who gave to each a numbered ticket, and inscribed their names on a register; while another official allotted to each a table, and distributed paper, ink, and pencils. In their impatient anxiety our two heroes had come early; but from the noise and excitement which began immediately to echo on every side of them, it was plain that there were very many others who were minded to be in good time also. At length, when every table was full, and every ticket given away, a drum was sounded, the folding-doors were closed, and the competitors were cut off from the outer world for the rest of the day. Presently the prefect entered at the upper end of the hall, and having taken his seat on a raised dais, thus addressed the assembled scholars :—

"You are all doubtless aware of the unusual circumstances under which I am holding this examination, and I take it for granted that you are cognisant of the prizes which are to be won by the two most successful competitors." Many an eye sparkled at this reference to the twins. "The two themes on which I shall ask you to write as many essays are taken from the ode of the 'Book of Poetry,' entitled 'The Tsin and the Wei.'" Here Te gave a great sigh of relief. "The first consists of the two opening lines—

> 'See where before you gleams the foaming tide
> Of Tsin and Wei down-sweeping in their pride;'

and the second, of what I may call the refrain of the ode—

> 'Beyond the watery waste of mighty Wei
> There blooms a garden rich in blossoms gay,
> Where lads and lasses toy in shady bowers,
> And pelt each other with soft-scented flowers.'

You will have observed that a secretary, who has been kindly lent me for the occasion by the Viceroy of the province, took down your names at the door, placing them on his scroll opposite the numbers corresponding with those on your tickets. Having finished your essays, you will be good enough to sign at the foot of each the number on your tickets—not your names. After the papers have been examined, and the order of merit arranged, this sealed envelope which I hold in my hand, and which contains the secretary's scroll, will be opened, and the names of the winners ascertained and announced. As the task of going over the essays will be a long one, I propose to proclaim the award on the fifteenth of the present month at noon. And now to your tasks. The prizes offered you are well worth a struggle, and I cannot imagine any objects more calculated to stir the blood and fire the imaginations of young men like yourselves than the lovely daughters of Ma."

"Oh, there is Te!"

When the students had settled down to their work, the prefect, acting on a sudden impulse, sent to invite the twins to look down at the competitors from the latticed gallery which ran along one side of the courtyard. Such an opportunity of looking down upon five hundred possible husbands was not to be lost, and as quickly as their chair coolies could carry them they presented themselves at the door of the private apartments. The prefect, who had grown quite alert when Daffodil and her sister were in question, snatched a moment from his duties in the hall to escort them to the gallery. Once alone they eagerly scanned the five hundred for the lineaments of their lovers.

"Te is in difficulties."

"Oh, there is Te!" said Daffodil. "I know him by the lie of his pigtail."

"Where do you mean?" asked Convolvulus, seeing

that her sister was looking in quite another direction to the one in which her eyes had been riveted for some minutes.

"In the front row, and about the tenth from this end."

"Why, you silly thing, there the dear fellow is, sitting in the fourth row, with his sleeves tucked up and his spectacles on."

"Well, then, all I can say is, that there is another young man with a pigtail exactly like Te's. Do you see Tsin?" she added, after a pause. "He is writing as though his life depended on it, and smiling at times as though some happy thoughts were crossing his mind."

"Oh!" exclaimed Convolvulus presently, "Te is in difficulties. He is biting the end of his pencil, as he always does when he is stranded for want of matter. I wish I were by him to encourage him."

"I don't think your presence would be likely to add much to the concentration of his thoughts," remarked her sister.

"Oh, there, he is off again! I wonder what thought suggested itself to him at that moment. Do you know, I sometimes think that Te and I are able to communicate mentally by speechless messages, for I have several times found that we have both been thinking of the same thing at the same moment."

"Oh, wonderful, wonderful, wonderful! But now we must be going, or those men near us will hear us chattering." So sending a dutiful farewell to the prefect, they returned home to await the arrival of their lovers, who had promised to report progress after the

"THEY LEANED OVER TO GREET THEIR LOVERS."—*Page 120.*

labours of the day. As the shades of evening fell, the sound of well-known footsteps brought the sisters to the balcony of the summer-house, and as they leaned over to greet their lovers, the young men instinctively paused to admire the beauty of the picture they made. Their light and graceful forms, clothed with all the taste and brilliancy of richly embroidered robes, and their exquisite features lit up with pleasure and expectancy, presented a foreground which found fitting surroundings in the quaint carving of the arbour and the masses of wistaria-blossom, which drooped like bunches of grapes from the eaves and every coign of vantage.

"Well?" they asked.

"Good news," was the answer. "The prefect was as good as his word, and everything turned out exactly as we had expected."

"That is capital. But we were sorry you did not sit together," said Daffodil.

"How do you know that we did not?" said Tsin, with surprise.

"And why, Te, did you tuck up your sleeves, as though you were going to contend with a sword, rather than with a pen?" said Convolvulus.

"Now, who told you that I tucked up my sleeves? Confess, or I'll——"

"Oh, what a pair of unsympathetic mortals you are!" broke in Daffodil, who was too happy to be silent. "There were we looking down upon you from the latticed gallery, and you were no more conscious of our presence than if you had been made of stone."

"And, Te, dear," said Convolvulus, "once when

your ideas had evidently forsaken you, I longed to be at your side to help you out. And I think my longing wish must have been of some use, for almost immediately you set to work again."

"Let us go for a stroll in the garden, and we will talk it all over," was the reply of the enamoured Te.

The ten days which elapsed between the examination and the announcement of the results passed slowly with Tsin and Te, and were mainly occupied in going over each point they had made and each opportunity they had missed. In the preliminary studies Tsin had among other points striven to impress upon Te the importance of drawing a comparison between the effect of the licentious music of the state of Ching, as illustrated by the manners of the people described in the ode, and that produced by the austere strains of Wei. But when the moment came for the use of this comparison, Te found himself hopelessly confused, and ended by attributing to the exceptionally pure airs of Wei an impropriety which bordered on grossness.

The recollection of this and other shortcomings weighed heavily on Te's spirits, and tortured him even in the presence of his lady-love.

"But what matters it," said that young lady, "if you do fail in one direction, so long as you make up for it in others? It is no use making a bridge wider than the river."

"True," replied Te; "but what if an architect puts his materials together so badly that they topple over into the stream?"

"What should you say of an architect," answered

Convolvulus, "who built a good bridge, and could not sleep of a night if a leaf stirred for fear it should be blown down?"

"Well, my eyes will not now be long 'blackened with the pencil of sleeplessness,' to use your own pretty imagery," answered her lover. "And I really don't know whether to wish that between this and the fifteenth Time should fly or move with leaden feet. At all events, I enjoy your presence now, and it may be that then it will be lost to me for ever."

"I should not give up hope even if you failed," replied the cheery little Convolvulus. "There are more ways of catching a bird than grasping his tail."

The intense anxiety felt by Tsin and Te as to their success or failure caused them, as perhaps was only natural, to lose sight, to a certain extent, of the fact that to the young ladies there was even more depending on the fifteenth than to themselves; for, after all, their failure would only bring on them a negative misfortune, while it was within the bounds of possibility that Daffodil and Convolvulus might find themselves bound to partners whom they loathed. The twins' interest in the day was heightened by the arrival of the prefect on the afternoon of the fourteenth, to invite them to be present on the following morning.

"I have arranged," said he, "a pretty little alcove on one side of the hall, where you can sit with your mother and watch the proceedings. As you know, I inserted a saving clause into my proclamation, reserving to myself the right of rejecting any student who should appear physically unworthy of you; and it may be that I may wish to refer the decision on such a delicate point to yourselves."

"How thoughtful you are, your Excellency! But I am sure we may trust you not to give us pock-marked, bald, or stunted husbands," said Daffodil, smiling.

"Now describe your idea of what a husband should be," replied the prefect.

"First of all, he must be tall," answered Daffodil, drawing a mental picture of Tsin, "with broad shoulders and an upright figure. He should have a well-formed nose, a bright eye, and a glossy pigtail."

"Just what I used to be in bygone days," thought the prefect to himself. Somehow lately he had taken to wishing that life was beginning with him anew, and after each interview with the twins he had returned to regard Madam Lo's matronly figure with increasing disfavour. On this particular occasion he was evidently bent on enjoying himself, and seemed disposed to reproduce in Ma's garden the free and easy manners of the frequenters of the "shady bowers" "beyond the watery waste of mighty Wei." Nothing loath, the girls indulged his humour, and when he finally took his leave he carried off with him one of Daffodil's prettily enamelled hairpins and Convolvulus's bangle.

On the following morning the town was early astir, and quite a crowd collected at Ma's doorway to see the twins start for the prefect's *yamun*. In that usually decorous building the scene was tumultuous. Not only did the five hundred competitors present themselves, but when it became known that the beautiful twins would be present, nearly the whole male population of the town, including myself, poured into the courtyard. The police and lictors had no light task in keeping order; and when the twins stepped into the alcove a rush was made to that side of the courtyard, which threatened to break down the barrier that enclosed the hall. Even the sounding of the drum and the appearance of the prefect produced little or no effect on the disorder which prevailed; and it was not until two or three of the most obtrusive admirers of the two beauties had been seized and flogged on the spot, that sufficient silence was obtained to allow of the opening of the proceedings.

"I have read," said the prefect, addressing the competitors, "with the greatest care the essays which you handed in on the fifth, and after much consideration I have selected two sets as being the best of those contributed by bachelors, and two whose authors are married men. As there is less to say about the married men, I will dispose of them first. I find that Ping and Lung are the winners in that competition. Let Ping and Lung step forward. Your essays," said the prefect, addressing the two scholars, "are extremely creditable, and I have much pleasure in presenting you with the gazelles which I advertised as your reward. I am only sorry for you that they are not the gazelles on my left hand," pointing to the twins.

"Most cordially do we echo your regret, your Excellency," said Ping, casting longing eyes towards the alcove; "but failing those priceless prizes, we thank you for the gifts you have conferred upon us.

"Now," said the prefect, "I come to the bachelors."

At these words there was a movement and excitement in the hall, which showed how deeply the admiration of the competitors had been stirred by the unparalleled beauty of the two sisters. To both Tsin and Te the moment was one of supreme concern. Tsin held his breath and bit his lip, while Te wrung his perfectly dry pocket-handkerchief as though it had been used, as well it might have been, to wipe the perspiration from off his streaming forehead.

"With regard to the winner of the first prize," he added, "I have no hesitation in pronouncing my decision. Beyond compare the essays of Tsin, in whom I am glad to recognise the son of an old friend, are infinitely the best. Not only do they display originality of thought and brilliancy of diction, but the depth of the scholarship they manifest is perfectly wonderful. I could not have believed that any scholar could have possessed so minute and accurate a knowledge of the writings of the scholiasts of all ages. I have known men who have been thoroughly acquainted with the critics of the Chow dynasty; others with those of the Han dynasty; others, again, with those of the T'ang dynasty;—but never have I met with any who had mastered so thoroughly the writings of all of them. And it becomes almost bewildering when one thinks that his knowledge of the scholia on every other ode in the 'Book of Poetry' is as perfect as his knowledge of the commentaries of this one. For why should I suppose that his attention has been especially attracted to this ode? Without question, then, I give the palm to Tsin. But with regard to the second prize I confess to have been in some doubt. However, after mature consideration, I have determined to award it to a gentleman of the name of Te." Here Convolvulus, who had been leaning forward to catch every word, threw herself back in her chair with a sigh of relief. "The genius," went on the prefect, "displayed by Tsin is wanting here, and there is a lack of literary ease, and sometimes a confusion of thought which has surprised me; but at the same time I cannot overlook the fact that, like Tsin, Te possesses an extraordinarily accurate knowledge of the ancient commentators. His power of quotation is prodigious, and it would almost seem that he had learnt the commentaries by heart. Proof of such untiring diligence and of such a wonderful memory may not be passed over, and I therefore proclaim Te the winner of the second prize. Tsin and Te stand forth."

With some trepidation the two young men stepped forward and made a profound bow to the prefect, who rose and went over to the twins.

"Do these young men satisfy your requirements, young ladies?" asked the prefect, smiling on them.

"Exceedingly well, your Excellency," said Daffodil.

Then returning to his seat, the prefect continued—

"To you, O most fortunate Tsin, the fates have awarded the incomparable Daffodil; while to your lot, Te, falls the equally matchless Convolvulus. Ascend the dais and let me introduce you to your brides."

With alacrity the young men mounted the steps and advanced towards the alcove. At the moment that they made their bow and swore their fealty, the band, which the prefect had provided for the occasion, struck up the well-known wedding air, "The Phœnixes in concord sing," and the courtyard rang with the shouts of "Good!" "good!" "Very good!" "good!" "good!"

After a short pause, caused by the difficulty of getting Ma and his wife to their appointed places in the hall, the happy couples made obeisance to heaven and earth, and to their parents; and then, with a deep reverence to the prefect, turned at his invitation towards the private apartments of the *yamun*, where, as I afterwards learned, he entertained them at a sumptuous feast. At the moment that the bridal procession passed from the hall the prefect turned to the crowd and said—

"I am quite aware that the course I have pursued on this occasion is an unusual one, and that it could only be justified by circumstances such as I was called upon to encounter. The result, however, has surpassed my highest expectations, and to-day we have seen two veritable dragons of learning united to beings of more than earthly beauty. Such a consummation is worthy the labours of the wisest of mankind, and reminds me of those well-known lines of the great poet of the T'ang dynasty—

'In all the regions watered by Hwang-ho
Or Yang-tse-Keang's current, tell me where
You'd find on sultry plain or mountain snow
Men half so wise or women half so fair?'"

A TWICE-MARRIED COUPLE.

"WELL, if I could make verses like you, and were as well up in the classics as you are, I should look for a wife among the families of the city merchants, and not throw myself away upon a cashless girl like Green-jade."

The speaker was a young man of the people, and of a forbidding aspect. His sallow cheeks were deeply marked with smallpox, his brow was overhanging, and his features were coarse and unintellectual. His dress was at the same time pretentious and dirty, and his manners were cringing and boisterous. The person addressed was a man of about his own age, but bore higher marks of culture than any displayed by Le Poko. Not that his appearance was by any means pleasing. His eyes were small and restless, his cheek-bones were abnormally high, his under lip protruded in a manner suggestive of meanness, and there was a general air of timidity and unrest about his gait. Le's remark evidently made an impression upon him. His eyes danced at the thought of the wealth and position which his friend's suggestion conjured up—for he was very poor, and was often dependent on kindly neighbours for his daily food. But presently a softening influence affected his expression.

"If you knew Green-jade as well as I do," he said to his friend, "you would not give such advice so readily. She has the beauty of Kinlien, the talents of Su Siao-siao, and all the virtues of the mother of Mencius. Added to which she is very fond of me, and would be content to keep house in a mat-shed and live on broken victuals, if I could make her my wife."

"And if, my dear Wang, you were to marry her, what would be your position? You would be unable to study, for you would not be able to buy the commonest books, and so all hope of advancement would be over for you. And to earn your bread you would be obliged to become either a common hawker of cheap goods, or a hanger-on at a mandarin's *yamun*. But if you were to take my advice, you might have a library at your disposal, powerful patrons to befriend you, and rich scholars to associate with. You would then be sure to win your way at the Examination Halls, and you might easily rise to a high post in the empire."

Le's mean advice was in accordance with the genuine instincts of his nature; but he had another motive in urging his friend to be faithless to Green-jade. Being the daughter of poor parents, Green-jade was unable to preserve the seclusion common to young ladies, and had not only made the acquaintance of Wang in the market-place and in the street, but had also occasionally chatted with Le. Not that she had any sympathy whatever with that graceless young man; but knowing that he was a friend of Wang—for whom, strange to say, she had formed a deep attachment—she was ready to be courteous to him. It is, however, a law of nature, that persons should be most attracted towards those of the opposite sex who possess qualities in which they themselves are deficient. And thus it came about that sensual, mean, coarse, and ignorant Le fell head and ears in love with the refined, intellectual, and graceful young person whom her parents had christened Green-jade, in recognition of her priceless value. He was not long in discovering, however, that Green-jade's affections were settled on his friend; nor had he any difficulty in finding out from Wang that what passed for his heart was given in exchange. Indeed the intercourse between the lovers had gone beyond the stage of chats in the market-place. Wang had of late been constantly in the habit of dropping in of an evening to see his neighbour Mr Chang, whose daughter would bring them tea and fill their pipes, while listening to their conversation on the wisdom of the ancients, the deep philosophy of the classics, and the soul-stirring poetry of the days of Confucius. To these things did Green-jade seriously incline, and with a greedy ear she devoured the discourse of the two scholars. It even sometimes happened that when her father was called away on household matters she would take up the theme, and Wang was charmed to find how just a literary taste was combined with the striking personal charms of his inamorata.

By degrees their chance interviews became less

classical and more personal. And though never crossing by one iota the boundary-line of strict propriety, Green-jade gave Wang evidences which were not to be misunderstood, that, if he would play the part of a Fêng, she would be willing to take the *rôle* of a Hwang.[1]

Such was the position of affairs when Le poured the poison of his advice into Wang's ears. Not on one occasion only but repeatedly he urged the same counsel, and even went the length of inquiring in the town for an heiress whose parents might be willing to link her fate with that of a promising scholar. Little by little his proposal, which had at first shocked Wang, became more palatable to him, and before long he even began to form schemes of work, and to dream of promotion won by the wealth of his rich bride. In this frame of mind he found visits to Chang's house distasteful, and he avoided meeting Green-jade as far as possible. Though he had enjoyed her company, he was incapable of feeling any deep affection for her. He was flattered by her evident liking and admiration for him, but beyond the sensation of gratified vanity, he had no sentiment towards her. With Green-jade, however, matters were very different. She had, with that wild infatuation which is common to imaginative young women, given her heart entirely to Wang, and she had become accustomed to regard his visits to her father as the bright spots in her existence. In her blind partiality

[1] The Fêng and Hwang are the male and female phœnixes which are regarded as emblems of bride and bridegroom.

she had entirely overlooked the meanness of his character, which was sufficiently obvious to less prejudiced observers. The discontinuance of his visits was therefore a grief and a surprise to her. Day after day she watched eagerly for his arrival. Every footfall raised her expectations, and her disappointment as they disappeared in the distance was in proportion to the depth of her longing.

With unnecessary scrupulousness she reproached herself with having done something to offend Wang, never imagining it possible that any fickleness on his part could account for the change; and even when rumours reached her — and Le took care that they should—that Wang was seeking to ally himself with a wealthy family in the neighbourhood, she still attributed his altered conduct to some fault of her own which she had unconsciously committed. With stern self-introspection she examined the whole course of her conduct from the time of her first acquaintance with Wang to find out wherein her fault lay, and wept bitter tears over words spoken and deeds done which she fancied might have given offence.

Meanwhile Le's agents had been busy, and had brought Wang a proposal which in some respects fulfilled his highest expectations. As in all large cities, the beggars in K'aifêng Fu were a numerous and powerful body. They exercised a social tyranny over the inhabitants, and habitually levied blackmail from them. If any one more daring than the rest ventured to resist their exactions, they invaded his dwelling or place of business, and kept up such a clatter with bells, broken dishes, and hollow bamboos, that he was soon obliged to yield to their demands. There was only one man to whom these lawless vagabonds yielded ready obedience. From time immemorial the chieftainship of the beggars of K'ai-fêng Fu had been vested in a certain Chu family which had grown rich on the dues paid by the individual beggars, and by the interest exacted on money lent to unfortunate members of the ragged army in times of need. So wealthy had the existing chief become, that he had for some time before the period at which our story opens ceased to take any active part in the administration of the beggar clan, and having no son, had delegated his authority to a nephew, known as "the Leper," from the fact of his having unfortunately contracted that disease in pursuit of his calling.

Chu had been early left a widower, with one daughter, of whom he was dotingly fond. Her slightest wish was eagerly attended to, and in all household matters her word was law. She was pretty also, and though not highly cultured she possessed many pleasant qualities. She was generous, affectionate, and bright-humoured, and was highly popular among her associates.

So soon as she arrived at a marriageable age, her father sought to find her a suitable husband among the young men of the city. Being rich, he thought that he might naturally expect to ally her with a youth of the official class, and accordingly employed a go-between, a certain Mrs Kin, to search out one who should be worthy of her. The go-between, who had a better appreciation of the position than Chu, undertook the mission with many doubts, which were confirmed when the parents of one and all declined with scorn to connect their son with so meanly born a maiden.

It was just as she had received a rebuff from the wife of the district magistrate, whose son had originally been low down in the list which Chu had given her, that Le's proposal on behalf of Wang reached her. The suggestion appeared to her to be a reasonable one, but she felt that some diplomacy would be required to reconcile Chu to the idea. There was a wide difference between the son of a mandarin and the penniless son of a deceased small shopkeeper, who though clever, it is true, had yet all his honours to win. It was with some trepidation, therefore, that she presented herself before Chu to report on her mission.

"Well, dame, what news have you for me?" inquired Chu as he greeted her.

"In some respects," replied Mrs Kin, "the Fates have been adverse, but they have been cruel only to be kind. It so happens that all those families you mention to me, from that of the Taotai downwards, are, for one reason or another, prevented, much to their annoyance," she added without a blush, "from accepting your most tempting offer. In some cases the young men were already engaged, in others ill health made marriage impossible, and in one or two instances I heard such dreadful accounts of the young men's manners of life that I suggested difficulties."

"So far the Fates seem to have been very adverse,"

said Chu; "but what have you to set on the other side of the account?"

"Why, then," replied the go-between, "just as I had begun to think that I should have but a poor account to give of my negotiation, I happened to meet a Mr Le, who is himself a no mean scholar, and who mentioned to me casually that a young bachelor friend of his, who is as learned as Chu Hi and as loftily-minded as Confucius, was anxious to ally himself with a lady who might be fitted in all respects to share the greatness which unquestionably awaits him, so soon as he shall have passed his examinations."

"And who is this paragon?" asked Chu.

"His name is Wang," said Mrs Kin, "and most appropriately is he so called,[1] for he is made to rule. The only thing against him is that at present he is poor; but if you consent to bestow your honoured loved one upon him you will cure that fault, and will give wings to this butterfly which will enable him to fly at once to the summit of the mountain of honour."

"What is his parentage?"

"His father," replied the go-between, "was a trader, and unfortunately died before he had made that fortune which would have inevitably been his if the Fates had not snapped his thread of life. On his mother's side he is related with a very distinguished family in Peking, one member of which now holds office in the Board of War; and another would have doubtless succeeded to great honour, had not

[1] *Wang* means to rule.

some colleagues, jealous of his rising fame, accused him of treason, and so turned the Dragon countenance against him that he was most unjustly beheaded."

"Dear, dear! that was unlucky," said Chu, who, in face of the non-success of his first proposals, began to take kindly to Mrs Kin's overtures. "But tell me something of this young man's personal appearance."

"To be quite truthful with you," replied Mrs Kin, who constantly employed this kind of adjuration when she spoke the truth, in order to give an air of authenticity to her statements generally, "I have not seen him yet. But if Mr Le, who has honesty stamped on his face if ever man had, is to be believed, he is as handsome as one of the eight immortals."

"It is a pity that his circumstances are so poor," said Chu, anxious not to seem over-desirous for the match.

"What is there in that?" said Mrs Kin. "Was not Kwan Ti[1] a seller of bean-curd in early life? And was not Han Sin,[2] when young, so poor that he was obliged to obtain sustenance by angling for fish in a castle moat?"

Overwhelmed by these historical allusions, Chu gave way, and commissioned Mrs Kin to consult a soothsayer as to the agreement of the Mêntanghu (family relationships) on either side. Pleased with her success, Mrs Kin went direct to Wang and com-

[1] Kwan Ti, a celebrated general who was canonised as the God of War.

[2] Han Sin, a statesman who was created Prince of Ts'u.

municated to him the result of her interview. At the same time she enlarged on the immense wealth of the lady's family, and the beauty and accomplishments of Miss Pearl. Wang was secretly delighted with her news, but was shrewd enough to appear indifferent.

"I am sure," he said, "I am very grateful to you for the interest you have taken in this matter. But unfortunately my circumstances are not such as would enable me to make the necessary wedding-presents, and I propose, therefore, to put off all thoughts of marriage until I have won my way to office."

"If Miss Pearl were an ordinary young lady, I should applaud your prudence," answered Mrs Kin; "but, as a matter of fact, she is one in ten thousand, a stork among poultry, a sun among stars, and to neglect the chance of an alliance with her is to fly in the face of the gods. And as to the wedding-presents, do not bestow one moment's thought upon them. I will arrange that they shall be as handsome as any that the Prefect's daughter got yesterday, and that you shall not be asked for a single cash on account of them until your pockets are overflowing with Miss Pearl's taels."

"On those conditions I am, if the lady is all you describe her to be, ready at least that you should open negotiations on the subject."

With this consent Mrs Kin took her leave, and lost no time in consulting a soothsayer on the prospects of the match. As she was able to promise a liberal fee, the result of her conference with the deities coincided exactly with her wishes. The next full moon was the time indicated by the Fates for the marriage, and the happiness promised to the young people was such as was to surpass the common lot of men. Mr Chu made most liberal preparations for the ceremony; and a complaisant money-lender, who had many a time and oft advanced money in promotion of Mrs Kin's schemes, willingly lent the sum required by Wang to provide the wedding-gifts.

As the match was not a particularly brilliant one in a social point of view, Mr Chu determined that he would make up in magnificence for what was wanting in that respect. As the day approached his house became a scene of wild confusion. Upholsterers were at work in the reception-rooms, as well as in those the young couple were to occupy; presents for the bride came pouring in; and milliners, accompanied by coolies bearing loads of silks and satins, haunted Miss Pearl's apartments. That young lady looked forward to her bridal day with mingled feelings. She knew enough of life to know that the reports of professional go-betweens were not always to be believed, and that marriage was not always the state of bliss that it was commonly reported to be. At the same time, her ambition was stirred. She saw plainly, if her father did not, that her parentage was a fatal bar to a good marriage, and she felt that her only chance of escape from the stigma which was cast upon her by her father's calling lay in marrying a man who would win by his talents a position for himself in the State. The inquiries she made privately convinced her that Wang's abilities were such as to secure him an official appointment, and she determined that no expense should be spared to enable him to surround himself with rich and powerful friends.

Meanwhile the report which had reached Green-jade's ears of Wang's intended marriage was fully confirmed with every circumstance of time and place. The hope which she had cherished that he might yet return to his old intimacy at her father's house was crushed fifty times a-day by the rumours which reached her of the magnificent preparations which were being made at Mr Chu's, and of the bridal gifts which Wang was collecting for presentation to his bride. Little did the gossips know the misery which they were inflicting on the poor girl by the news they brought her, and much did they wonder that she turned away from their chatter without asking a single question about the bride and bridegroom. She never told her love, and struggled on through her daily employments with a heavy heart and a deepening sorrow. The light was taken out of her life. There were no longer any meetings and talks to look forward to, and there remained only a danger of her settling down into a condition of despair. Even her father, who was not an observant man, could not help noticing that she had lost all elasticity of manner, and putting it down to ill health, urged her to pay a visit to a relative living at Tsining, on the Grand Canal.

Fortunately at this juncture a letter came from the relative in question, asking Green-jade, for whom the writer had a great affection, to undertake the instruction of her little girl, her own health being unequal to the task. The proposal was accompanied by many expressions of kindness and regard, and a liberal remuneration was offered for the required service. The lady, a Mrs Ting, who was a cousin of Green-jade's father, had been fortunate enough to marry a man who was not only an excellent husband, but was also a man of great ability. With unusual rapidity he had risen through the lower grades of the public service, and was at the time of which we speak Prefect of Tsining. Green-jade, in the frame of mind in which she then was, eagerly welcomed the offer; and her father, though grieved at the idea of losing the society of his daughter, felt that it was an opportunity of providing for her which he ought not to refuse. The proposal was therefore accepted, and poor little Green-jade busied herself in making such preparations as it was within her means to compass.

The news of Green-jade's intended departure produced on Wang and Le very opposite effects. To Wang it was a relief to know that he would be no longer annoyed by the consciousness of her presence. He was not the least conscience-stricken for the part he had played, but it was disagreeable to him to witness the effect of his misconduct. But Le was in despair. With all the force possible to men of his coarse nature he loved Green-jade, and the idea of losing sight of her was misery to him. He had not intended urging his suit until after Wang's marriage, lest his treachery to his friend should become too apparent. But the turn which events had taken determined him to seek an interview with Chang at once. He was fortunate enough to find him alone.

"I hear," he said to his host, "that your 'honoured loved one' is preparing for a journey. May I ask if she is likely to be long absent from your palace?"

"My insignificant daughter," replied Chang, "has not been well of late, and I had proposed that she should pay a visit to the wife of the Prefect of Tsining, who is a relative of mine, when an invitation from that lady came, asking her to undertake the charge of her daughter. So that, in all probability, she will be away for some years."

"I have long watched your honoured daughter growing up like a fairy among her young companions, or like a phœnix among crows. I have admired her beauty, and have wondered at her learning. As you know, I have not yet 'established a family,' and it would overjoy me to receive your beloved one into my cold dwelling as my bride. May I ask 'my benevolent elder brother' how he regards my proposal?"

Chang had never liked Le, and he was well aware that his daughter shared in the same feeling: he had therefore no hesitation in declining the offer, more especially as he knew that Le's means were of the straitest, and that his modest description of his house was more in accordance with truth than his assertions commonly were. He replied therefore—

"Honoured sir, your proposal reflects glory on our humble family. But my daughter, having undertaken the charge of Prefect Ting's little one, cannot snatch the precious fruit which you so temptingly offer for her acceptance."

"But would it not be possible to decline the Prefect's proposal?" pleaded Le.

"I fear not," replied Chang; "and therefore, while I am much honoured by the proposal you have made, I am regretfully obliged to decline it."

Chang spoke in so positive a way that Le felt that it would be useless to press his suit further, and he therefore took his leave in a by no means enviable mood. Regret at losing Green-jade, whom he had regarded as a sure prize, was largely mingled with wounded vanity, and anger against Chang. For a time he even thought of kidnapping Green-jade when on her way to Tsining, but there were difficulties in the way, not the least of which was that arising from want of cash, and he eventually made up his mind to take every means in his power of revenging himself upon Chang, and of so humiliating him as to make him wish that he had given his consent to the match.

Meanwhile Green-jade's departure for Tsining was speedily followed by Wang's marriage to Miss Pearl. Every accessory which money could buy was provided to add lustre to this last ceremony. The procession of bridal presents on the evening before the wedding was a sight to be seen, and the street arabs pronounced it to be, without question, the finest thing of its kind that had been seen for many years in K'aifêng Fu. But these exterior splendours were entirely eclipsed by the sumptuous decoration of Chu's reception-rooms, and by the feast provided for the wedding guests. Wishing to do Wang every honour, Chu had begged him to ask all his associates to the entertainment; and Wang, desirous to mitigate his friends' sneers at his marriage by showing them the evidences of his father-in-law's wealth, took advantage of Chu's hospitality to invite all his fellow-students and literary acquaintances. But numerous as these were, there was plenty for them all. The tables literally groaned under the weight of the delicacies which were piled upon them. Birds' nests from the islands, venison from Mongolia, wine from Chekeang, pears and grapes from Shantung, and preserves from Canton, were provided in more than sufficient quantities to satisfy the appetites of the feasters, who, at the conclusion of the marriage ceremony and the retirement of the bride and her bridesmaids, were left to the full enjoyment of the luxuries before them.

Nor were the festivities entirely confined to the inside of the house, for in the street the arrival of the guests had caused a crowd to collect, among whom, by Chu's orders, cash and common viands were distributed. The news of this lavish expenditure quickly reached the beggars' headquarters. The Leper had been aware of the wedding, and supposing that it would be conducted quietly, had not cast a thought on the fact that he, as a kinsman, had not been invited. When, however, his emissaries brought him word that crowds of guests were pouring into Chu's wide-opened doors, and that the feast was almost a public one, he felt that he had been slighted. He was naturally of a touchy nature, and ill health had increased his infirmity.

"What does this proud cousin of mine mean," he exclaimed to a wretched beggar who had crawled in on crutches to tell him of the food and cash which were to be had outside Chu's house, "by ignoring me, his kinsman, and the beggars who have raised him to his present position of wealth, by not inviting us to his feast? The fact that his daughter is marrying one of the *literati* is no reason why he should turn his back on his relations and old associates."

"That was just what I was thinking as I came along," said the old beggar in a whining tone. "When I was told that you, honoured sir, were not among the guests, and that food and cash were being distributed without any notice having been sent to us, I could scarcely believe it. But now I have seen what is going on with my own eyes, or eye I *should* say," parenthetically remarked the old man with a grim smile, for he had long been blind on one side,—"and here," he said, fumbling in his scrip, "are some of the spoils I brought along with me."

"This is too bad," said the Leper, working himself up into a state of anger. "I will teach him that we are to be reckoned with, though we are beggars. Go," said he to the old cripple, "and call twenty men from the lodging-house, and we will give Chu some clatter which he won't forget in a hurry."

In obedience to this summons, the courtyard was speedily filled with a group of beings who represented every ill that flesh is heir to. The lame, the maimed, the halt, and the blind were all there, and with them victims to every form of disease. Nothing but rags and tatters covered the persons of these lazar-house inmates, while in the hands of each were bells, hollow bits of bamboo, horns, and whistles, besides the staffs which supported their tottering frames.

On this motley crew the Leper looked with pride. Though better dressed than the beggars, he was scarcely less repulsive-looking than they. The disease from which his nickname was derived had made strange havoc with his features. The skin of his face was lumpy and discoloured, and the irritation under which he was at the moment suffering had added a malignant expression to his afflicted countenance.

"This is too bad."

"Come with me to my cousin Chu's house," he cried, as he stepped into the courtyard, "and help me to give him a lesson in propriety. All the city are feasting at his table, and he has not had the decency either to invite me as a guest or to send us a present of flesh and wine. But I will give him and his friends some music which they will find it hard to dance to."

Thus saying, he led the way to Chu's house, and arrived just as the *convives* were toasting each other in wine, and asking and answering riddles, in accordance with the custom of wedding-feasts. As he and his troop entered the outer courtyard he gave the word to begin the riot, and instantly there rose a clamour which defies description. Imitations, and, to do the beggars justice, very good imitations, of dogs yelping, cats screeching, and cocks crowing, were mingled with the sound of bells, gongs, hollow bamboos, and whistles. Never out of Pandemonium had such discords been heard. At the first outbreak of the noise Chu dropped his cup and turned deadly pale, for he recognised at once the meaning of the disturbance. The guests, less instructed, thought it was the beginning of a mask or play devised for their entertainment, and looked with curiosity towards the door which separated them from the outer yard. They had not long to wait before it was thrown open, when, to their astonished gaze, the Leper at the head of his followers marched into their midst. Straight they walked up to the principal table, and while the Leper took the cup of wine out of Wang's hand, his troop, who were now silent, pounced greedily upon the viands which still encumbered the tables.

Involuntarily the guests slunk away from the intruders, while Chu, who had partly recovered his presence of mind, came forward, and with the best pretence of cordiality which he could assume, paid his compliments to the Leper.

"I am glad to see you, my honoured brother," he said, "and I should have written to invite you if I had not delegated my powers for the day to my new son-in-law. On the third day after the wedding I am to have my own feast, and you will get an invitation to that in due course. And now let me introduce my son-in-law to you." So saying, Chu turned to the place where Wang had been sitting, but his chair was empty. So were all the seats round the table, and Chu met the gaze of the Leper with a look of blank and astonished annoyance.

"Ha! ha!" cried the Leper, "your fine holiday guests seem as frightened of me as poultry are of a fox. Why, there is not one of them left; and as it is a pity that the table should remain empty, I and my mates will sit down and enjoy ourselves."

Suiting the action to the word, the Leper sat down in Wang's seat, and his noisome companions ranged themselves on the chairs which had been so recently occupied by the silk and satin friends of the bridegroom.

The circumstances were trying, but Chu did his utmost to maintain an outward show of pleasure, even when his mind was tortured with the thought that in the eyes of his son-in-law and his companions he was disgraced for ever. When his tattered guests had satisfied their hunger, which was not for a long time, he turned to the Leper and said—

"I trust that my benevolent elder brother will accept from me a present of food and wine for those other 'flowery ones'[1] who dwell in his palace, and who have not honoured my lowly cottage by their presence to-day."

[1] An expression for beggars.

"THE FLOWERY ONES."

"Pray, do not put yourself to so much trouble," replied the Leper. In spite of this gentle disclaimer, Chu ordered his attendants to take a goodly supply of the choicest fare to the Leper's house. The Leper now rose to take his leave.

"I fear we have put you to infinite trouble," said he, as he made his bow, "and that we have sadly disturbed your other guests. But, believe me, my object in coming was to show you that though poor and degraded, I have not lost all interest in my kinsfolk and relations."

"I am deeply indebted to you," said Chu, "for having directed the course of your chariot to my humble dwelling. Your condescension is engraven on the tablets of my heart, and I only regret that I had such poor fare to put before such honoured guests."

So soon as the last cripple had dragged his distorted limbs over the threshold, Chu hurried to his daughter's apartments to express to Wang his intense regret at the *contretemps*. To his surprise he found his daughter alone, weeping bitterly at the disgrace which had fallen on her. Wang, at the invitation of one of the guests, had taken refuge in a neighbouring house until the unwelcome intruders should have taken their departure. While Chu was explaining matters to his daughter Wang returned, and it was easy to see that, though outwardly polite, he was greatly annoyed at the incident. He accepted Chu's apologies with courtesy, and that worthy was fain to leave to his daughter's charms and the advantages of the wealth now at his disposal the task of gradually obliterating the sense of shame which was plainly uppermost in the mind of his son-in-law. And to some extent, as time went on, these influences had their effect.

Miss Pearl did all she could to soothe and amuse her husband; and to one who had been accustomed all his life long to grinding poverty, the pleasure of having as many taels at command as he had formerly had cash brought a sensation of comfort and relief, which inclined him for a time to fall a satisfied victim to his bride's endearments.

His more liberal income enabled him also to surround himself with books, and by degrees his former fellow-students so far consented to forget the past as to join him in his study, and to cap verses with him over the excellent Suchow wine with which his father-in-law supplied him. By the help of these advantages Wang's scholarship received a finish which enabled him to compete successfully at the examinations, and by the influence of his friends his success was crowned by the receipt of an appointment to the post of commissariat officer to the brigade of troops stationed at Ch'ung K'ing on the Yangtsze-kiang.

There are some men in whom prosperity brings out into relief the worse points in their characters. Wang was one of these. So soon as the novelty of wealth had worn off, the consciousness that he was tied to the daughter of a beggar chieftain became more and more unendurable to him; and his sense of the advantages he had derived from the alliance was lost in regret that now that he was in a position to marry a lady of rank he was no longer able to do so. Le, who, like a true parasite, had allied himself more closely to Wang as that scholar had risen in the social scale, fostered these feelings for the double purpose of currying favour with his patron, and of avenging himself for some slight which he had suffered, or fancied he had suffered, at the hands of Pearl. So successfully had he wound himself into the good graces of Wang, that he received the appointment of private secretary to the new commissary, and embarked with his patron on the vessel which was to carry him to his post. Pearl took leave of her father with a heavy heart. The change which had come over her husband's demeanour towards her was of too marked a character to admit of any self-deception, and in leaving K'aifêng Fu she felt that she was putting herself entirely in the hands of a man whom she despised, and whose principles were nought. She was of a hopeful nature, however, and trusted to winning back her husband by devotion to his interests and attention to his whims and wishes.

The removal from Chu's house and influence produced an evil effect upon Wang's cowardly nature. He was one of those men with whom fear is the most potent influence, and with his freedom from his father-in-law's presence disappeared the conventional consideration with which he had been accustomed to treat his wife. He left her more and more to the society of her maid-servants, and spent the whole of the day in the company of his graceless secretary. Pearl, who was of an impressionable nature, longed frequently to get him to join in her admiration of the scenery through which they passed as they glided up the great river. But after one or two attempts she gave up trying to attract his attention, and sat silently wondering at the beetling cliffs of the gorges, and the whirling rapids which rushed through them. Accustomed as she was to the comparatively level country near K'aifêng Fu, the height of the mountains on either side, and the gloom of the passages, occasionally produced a feeling of awe and impending danger which quite unnerved her; and not unfrequently she was obliged to tell Peony, her maid, to shut out the sight by putting up the shutters of the boat.

To these terrors of the imagination was not unfrequently added the presence of real danger. On more than one occasion the rope by which the trackers were towing the boat over the rapids broke, and the craft was sent whirling down through the boiling water, and was only saved from destruction by the boatmen's skill in using the sweeps. After one such adventure in the Witches' Gorge the trackers had with infinite labour dragged the boat up through the foaming surges into the comparatively smooth water above. There they had anchored for the night, and for the first time that day Pearl ventured to look out on the scenery about her.

"How infinitely grand these mountains are!" she said to her faithful attendant, Peony, "but their size and gloom oppress me. I feel so strangely little and powerless in their presence."

"I am beginning to feel the same sensation myself," said Peony; "but all day long I have been watching the monkeys on the cliffs and the trackers on the towing-path, and I don't know which looked the most ridiculous. The monkeys were playing all sorts of antics, springing from crag to crag, fighting, throwing down stones into the river, and chattering all the while like a lot of magpies; while the men, who had no more clothes on than the monkeys, were jumping from rock to rock, tumbling into the water, and balancing themselves on narrow ledges, like so many boys at play. I wish you could amuse yourself as I do, but since we have been on the river you seem to have lost all interest in what is going on about you."

"I suppose I am not well," said Pearl, "but I feel a depression as of impending danger, and last night I dreamt that that old woman who told me my fortune in the Willow Garden last year appeared before me, and chanted again the doggerel couplet which I had quite forgotten until it came back to me in my dream. Do you remember it?—

'When witches' cliffs encircle you about,
Beware your fate; your sands are near run out.'

What do they call this gorge?"

"The Witches' Mountain gorge."

"Here, then, the fortune-teller's words will be put to the test. And if it is true that coming events cast their shadows before, this woman spoke with the inspiration of a seer."

"Oh, madam, you frighten me," said Peony, half inclined to cry; "please think no more about what that stupid old woman said. My father used to say in his joking way, 'All women are liars, and fortune-telling women are the greatest liars of all. They only say those things to mystify and amuse people.'"

"Well, time will show whether she was right or not. But I'm so weary that I shall go to bed, and try to forget in sleep the woman's prophecy and my own forebodings."

"And in the morning, madam, we will laugh over your fancies, and will begin the new day with fresh hopes. Who can say that a new life may not be opening to you to-morrow!"

"I would it might!—but come now and help me to undress."

Wang took no notice of his wife's retirement. For some time her comings and goings had been matters of complete indifference to him. On this particular evening, having dined heavily, he was lying in the forepart of the boat with Le, smoking opium. As had not been unusual of late, Wang's *mésalliance*, as he was good enough to call it, was the subject of their conversation, and Le drew many a glowing picture of the matches Wang might make were he but free. As the night wore on Le became more and more eloquent on the theme, unchecked by Wang, whose mean and covetous nature was all aglow at the imaginary prospects which his friend's words conjured up before him. At length Le's fancy failed him, and the two men lay inhaling their opium and enjoying the mental hallucinations which the drug provides for its votaries. Suddenly Le raised himself on his elbow, and said slowly—

"How the water rages and foams past the boat!

If any one were to fall overboard on such a night as this, they would be swept miles away before people would be aware of what had happened. No shriek would be heard in such a rushing stream, and the body would never be found in these countless eddies and whirlpools."

Wang turned sharply round at these words and gazed into Le's face. But that worthy avoided his eye, and appeared to be absorbed in watching the water lashing itself against a boulder-rock which stood out of the river, unmoved by the waves which leapt over it and the current which gurgled round it.

"What do you mean?" he said, in a deep excited voice.

"Nothing," said Le. "But I am going to bed. Good night." So saying, Le sauntered off, but turned as he reached the cabin door and cast one glance at Wang, who had followed his retreating form with a feverish gaze. Presently that worthy rose, inflamed by wine and evil passion, and paced excitedly up and down the deck. Then he looked out upon the waters, and walking carefully along the edge of the boat, removed a temporary taffrail which had been put in the forepart of the vessel. His hand shook so that he accomplished it with difficulty. He next assured himself that the sailors and servants were all asleep, and then went to his wife's room. He pushed back the door and called "Pearl."

"Who is that?" shrieked Pearl, who awoke startled from her sleep, and failed to recognise her husband's voice, so hollow and quivering it was.

"It is I, your husband," said Wang; "come out and look at the moon shining on the river."

Such an invitation sounded so strange to Pearl that she was delighted and rose at once, and began to hope that Peony was a truer prophet than the fortune-teller. But when by the light of the moon she saw Wang's face, a horrible presentiment came over her. She shuddered all over as with cold.

"I won't come out on to the deck," she said, "the night air is so chill, and I can see perfectly here."

"Nonsense," said Wang, seizing hold of her arm; "you must come when I tell you."

"Your looks frighten me," she cried, trembling. "Why do you look so pale, and why do your eyes glare so? But if I must come, let me call Peony to bring me a cloak."

"Call Peony! call the devil!" he said, as he dragged her to the prow.

"Oh, have mercy upon me!" said poor Pearl, as she struggled vehemently to get free. "Only let me go, and I will promise to do everything you wish, and will serve you as a dog his master. Or if you want to get rid of me, I will go home to my father. Have pity on me, and spare my life!"

"Hold your tongue, and stand here!" cried Wang, as he supported her almost fainting form near the edge of the boat.

"Oh, you can't be so cruel as to mean to kill me! Have pity, have mercy upon me!"

For a moment Wang's face seemed to soften, but only for a moment. With a wild glance he looked round to see that no one was about, and then tearing poor little Pearl's arms from his neck, round which she had thrown them in her misery, he hurled her into the torrent.

With one piercing shriek, and one wild reproachful look, she sank beneath the surface. Almost instantly she rose again into sight, and was then swept away by the force of the current into the distance. Wang had not the nerve to watch her fate, and to listen to her screams, but ran into the cabin and closed the door on the outer world. In a few minutes, which seemed to him like hours, he crept out and gave one hasty glance over the broken, foaming waters astern of the boat. No sign of his victim was visible, and he went back and threw himself on his bed. Sleep was out of the question. His wife's last shriek rang again and again in his ears, and whenever he closed his eyes her face rose up before him out of the darkness, after an instantaneous consciousness that it was coming, in a way which made rest impossible. Once or twice in the night he went on deck to cool his brow, but the sight of the spot on the boat where he had done the deed, and of the waters which held his secret, was too much for him, and he crept back again to bed.

At earliest dawn he awoke the captain of the boat, and ordered him to push on at once. The man, though half asleep, could not but be struck with the deathlike look of Wang's face; but, putting it down to the wine and opium of the night before, made no remark. The noise of the sailors moving about was an infinite relief to Wang, and he began to picture to himself what they would say, and how Peony would

"With one piercing shriek . . . she sank beneath the surface."

behave when Pearl's disappearance became known. This made him think what part he ought to play in the matter. So soon as he could bring his thoughts to bear on the subject, he determined to let Peony make the discovery when she went to her mistress's cabin in the morning, and to profess complete ignorance of the event, allowing it to be supposed that it was a case of suicide.

At his wife's usual hour for rising he heard Peony go to her cabin, and afterwards out on to the deck. Presently she returned, and seemed to be making a search, and then he heard her hurry off as fast as her small feet would carry her to the servants' part of the boat. Almost immediately his valet came to his cabin.

"Your Excellency," said the man, "Peony cannot find my lady; she has searched everywhere for her. But what is the matter, sir?" he added, as he saw Wang's blanched and terror-stricken face; "has anything happened?"

"Why, you fool," said Wang, "you tell me yourself that something has happened, when you say that your lady cannot be found. Help me to dress."

Help was indeed needed. Wang was so completely unnerved that he was scarcely able to stand.

"Shall I bring your Excellency some opium?" suggested the man, seeing his condition.

"Yes, quickly."

The materials for a pipe of the drug were always at hand in Wang's household, and before many minutes had elapsed he was stretched on the divan greedily inhaling the "foreign dirt." Gradually under the soothing influence of his pipe his eyes lost their wild excited look, his features relaxed, and his hand recovered some of its steadiness. While thus engaged, Le came in and expressed concern at the disappearance of Pearl. He just glanced at Wang with a strange inquiring look, and then turned away.

"Come and help me search for her," said Wang, who had now partly recovered his composure.

Together the pair went out to go through the form of looking for one of whose fate they were equally well informed, for Le had watched the struggle on the deck through his cabin window, and had heard Pearl's wild despairing shriek as she disappeared overboard.

Peony was heart-broken when it became apparent that Pearl was not in the boat. The tone of her mistress's remarks on the previous night suggested to her mind the idea of suicide, and this being repeated to Wang by his valet, brought some degree of relief to the terror-stricken mind of the murderer. The idea of searching in the troubled waters of the rapids was obviously futile, and no halt was therefore made in the progress up-stream. As the day wore on Wang regained his calmness under the influence of opium and the consciousness of personal safety. The sailors noticed that he never went to the forepart of the boat as had been his wont; and Peony took a strange and unaccountable aversion to him, which she was quite unable to repress. Thus the days wore on in the gloom-surrounded boat, and it was an infinite relief to all when at the end of a week they ran alongside the wharf at Ch'ung K'ing.

Meanwhile the same fair wind of promotion which

had made Wang Commissary at Ch'ung K'ing had brought the rank of Intendant of Circuit at the same place to Ting, the Prefect of Tsining. By a further chance the Commissary's boat was only the length of the rapid ahead of that of his superior officer. And on the particular night on which poor Pearl was thrown overboard, Ting, his wife, and Green-jade, were sitting on deck enjoying the beauty of the moon, and watching the foaming waters which came rushing down ahead of them. While thus sitting they were startled by a woman's cry coming from the broken water of the rapid. Such an alarm was no uncommon thing at that spot. Scarcely a day passed but some boat was upset, or some tracker lost his precarious footing and fell into the flood. The watchman on the police boat, which was moored close to Ting's, took the incident as a matter of course. Not so Ting, who, not being accustomed to these stern alarums, rushed to the head of the boat armed with a boat-hook, and eagerly looked out over the rushing waters. Another wild scream drew his attention to a direction in which he dimly descried a living object being borne rapidly along towards his boat. With nervous energy he awaited its approach, and as it passed he deftly caught the dress of the woman, as it now turned out to be, with the boat-hook. Mrs Ting and Green-jade stood by breathless, watching his manœuvres; and as he dragged the sufferer alongside, they caught hold of her, and by their united efforts pulled her on board.

"Is she alive?" asked Green-jade, pale and trembling with excitement.

"She was a minute or two ago," said Mrs Ting. "But don't waste time by asking questions. Chafe her hands while I rub her chest, and maybe she will recover."

"I hope I did not make that bump on her forehead," put in Ting.

"No, you did not touch her face," said his wife; "that must have been done by a blow against one of the rocks in the river. See! she breathes. I am so glad. Now, if we can only get her comfortably to bed, we may bring her round. Do you carry her to Green-jade's bed, and I will get her wet clothes off, poor thing."

Tenderly Ting bore the apparently lifeless form to Green-jade's cabin, and left her to the care of the two women.

That she was alive was all that could be said, and it was hours before she woke to consciousness.

"Where am I?" she murmured, as she opened her eyes.

"With friends," answered Green-jade, "who are going to take care of you until you are quite well. And now take a little of this hot wine which I have for you."

"He did not mean to do it," she wandered on, having taken Green-jade's kindly dose; "I am sure he did not. It was an accident—quite an accident;" and having said this, she dropped off into a sound sleep.

From an inspection of Pearl's clothes, Mrs Ting and Green-jade had come to the conclusion that she belonged to the official class; but it was late the next day before she was sufficiently coherent to explain her immersion. With this explanation, in which she did all she could to shield her husband, came the announcement of who she was, and Green-jade recognised in her the bride of her faithless lover. By degrees the whole truth came out, partly in consequence of the explanation required to account for her rooted objection to return to her husband, and partly in response to the confidences which Green-jade imparted to her. A warm attachment sprang up between the two women, which had for its central point their abhorrence of Wang's ungrateful and cruel conduct. Before they reached Ch'ung K'ing they had sworn eternal sisterhood; and Ting, in whose eyes also Pearl had found favour, had formally adopted her as his daughter.

The fact of the rescue was kept a profound secret outside the boat, and Ting, his wife, and Green-jade were the only people who were aware of Pearl's identity. On landing at Ch'ung K'ing, Pearl went with the other ladies of the household to the Intendant's *yamun*, and not a word was breathed as to the way in which she had entered their household.

The first duty Ting had to perform was to make the acquaintance of his subordinates, and amongst others that of Wang. That gentleman had not quite recovered from the shock to his nerves occasioned by the tragedy in the boat, and indeed it had been prolonged by the heavy doses of opium which he had since been in the habit of taking. His appearance as he presented himself before his superior officer was not prepossessing. His usual forbidding features were distorted by mental disquiet and blurred by the effects of stimulants. For some few seconds, as he made his bows, he was unable to speak coherently, and even when seated beside his host he found Ting's searching gaze so disconcerting that he had great difficulty in expressing himself. Altogether, Ting's report to his wife of his interview was not in Wang's favour, although he had to admit that one or two classical allusions which he had succeeded in making showed a scholarly training.

Before Pearl had been domesticated at the Intendant's *yamun* many days she opened communication with Peony through a discreet servant, who brought that faithful maid to the *yamun*, without divulging by the way more than was absolutely necessary. Peony's surprise and delight when she saw her mistress safe and sound were overwhelming. She cried and laughed, and became quite hysterical in her joy. But the account she brought of the life which she and her fellow-voyagers had led for some days after the eventful night was terrible. Wang's condition she described as having been little short of madness. His temper had been to the last degree irritable, and any sudden noise or unexpected intrusion into his presence had produced uncontrolled outbursts of anger. Le's influence had, according to Peony, greatly increased, and Wang evidently stood in awe of him. Suspicions of foul play had been generally entertained, and an air of doubt and reticence had pervaded the vessel.

As time wore on, however, Wang's mental and physical condition improved. He settled down to his new work at Ch'ung K'ing with zeal and diligence, finding in active employment the best antidote against the reproaches of his conscience. Though having a profound contempt and dislike for him, Ting was compelled to admit that he showed considerable administrative ability in the discharge of his duties. The one fault which his superior officer had to find was that he permitted Le to levy blackmail on contractors and tradesmen in virtue of his official position. Repeated remonstrances on this subject produced no effect, Wang being afraid to offend or get rid of a man who, he instinctively felt, knew so much. At length Ting was obliged to take the matter into his own hands, and finding a strong case against the offender, he threw him into prison, and thus made it impossible for Wang any longer openly to support him.

Meanwhile rumours reached Ting that Wang was again contemplating marriage. He announced himself as a widower; and as his official position and future prospects were decidedly good, his appearance in the matrimonial market made quite a stir among the ladies at Ch'ung K'ing. This gave Ting an opportunity of carrying out a scheme which he had long had in his mind. He had felt for some time that if Wang and his wife could be brought together again in circumstances which would secure her against a repetition of wrong, it was his duty to arrange it. It now occurred to him that if he could, by offering Wang his wife in remarriage under the guise of his adopted daughter, bring this about, it would destroy the principal motive which had actuated Wang in the commission of his crime, and would give Pearl a position which would make any ill-usage on his part impossible. After consultation with his wife, he asked Pearl to give him an interview in his study.

"Your position," he said, "has long been a cause of anxiety to me. If anything were to happen to me, you would be obliged to return to your father, and then all the circumstances connected with your tragedy would necessarily become public property. The only way out of the difficulty, so far as I can see, is that you should marry again."

"How can you, of all men in the world, propose such a thing to me? Don't you know that a faithful minister can serve only one sovereign, and a virtuous wife only one husband?"

"I expected some such answer from you. But what should you say if I married you, my adopted daughter, to Commissary Wang, who is, as I have reason to believe, looking out for a wife to supply the place of his dear departed?"

"What! remarry my own husband, and one who has attempted to murder me? Impossible."

"He attempted to murder you because you were a beggar chieftain's daughter: now you are the daughter of the Intendant of Ch'ung K'ing. He felt safe in doing it because he knew that you had no official influence, but he would not dare now to touch a hair of your head."

"But I have a horror of him."

"Remember, also, you have a duty towards him. If you let him marry some one else, what will the position of both of you be? Think it all over, and come to me again when you have made up your mind."

Deeply Pearl pondered the matter, and long were the consultations which she held on the subject with Mrs Ting, Green-jade, and Peony. Dutifully Mrs Ting advised the course recommended by her husband. Green-jade's advice was less pronounced, and Peony was loud in her expressions of horror at the idea.

"Why, if, after once having escaped from his cruelty, you were to tempt fortune again, you would be like the rat in the fable, who, having got out of the trap with the loss of his tail, went back and lost his head. Besides, a wife ought at least to like her husband, and how could you ever endure a man who has tried to mur——"

"Hush," said Pearl, "you must not talk in that way. And did you never hear of Lady Le, the wife of an officer in Wu-te's court, who recovered the affections of her husband after years of cruel estrangement, by devotion and self-sacrifice?"

"No, I never did; and I can never believe that it can be the duty of any one to outrage nature to such an extent. Before I could go back to a man who had treated me as the Commissary has treated you, I would take an overdose of laudanum, or go on a voyage to England, or do anything else desperate in its folly."

In spite, however, of Peony's eloquence, Pearl eventually agreed to accept Ting's advice, and that gentleman arranged that his secretary should make it known privately to Wang that a proposal on his part for the hand of the Intendant's adopted daughter would be favourably received. Wang was delighted at the hint. He felt that such a marriage would put him at once at an advantage. Already Ting's position was illustrious, and his abilities and influence were such that it was beyond question that before long he would be within reach of the highest offices of the State. How different, he thought, was his present condition from that in which he had been glad to marry the beggar chief's daughter! Filled with delight at the prospect before him, he lost no time in opening negotiations, and had just sent off the bridal presents, when a note from Ting informed him that, owing to his wife's serious illness, the marriage would have to be postponed. A few days later a further notice reached him of the fatal conclusion of the illness. "The Fates," wrote Ting, "have snapped the thread of her life, and I am left alone like a stork in the desert. I fear that it will be necessary for you to postpone plucking the plum-blossom [1] for a while."

Wang was loud in his condolences, and was quite content to wait, so long as he felt sure of the alliance. Indeed the affliction which had overtaken Ting was rather gratifying to him than otherwise. The sudden death of so great a lady was naturally a subject of general gossip, and the reflected notoriety which Wang enjoyed, as the intended son-in-law of the deceased, pleased him not a little. He waited patiently, therefore, during the six months required of him, and was not the least annoyed when he received an intimation, towards the end of that time,

[1] A poetical expression for marrying.

that for certain private reasons the Intendant wished for a still further postponement for three months. The fact being that, for the due management of his household, he was about, as he told Wang in confidence, "to take as my second wife a relative of the late Mrs Ting, one Green-jade, who, for some time, has been a member of my household, and who is in happy possession of all the virtues." He further proposed that the two weddings should take place on the same day, when, as he wrote, "in the words of the great T'ang poet—

'Two happy pairs shall taste the richest joy,
And welcome pleasure 'reft of all alloy.'"

To this proposal Wang readily assented. To share a marriage-feast with so high and exalted an officer as the Intendant filled his soul with delight. He revelled in the thought of the contrast between his condition as a poor penniless scholar at K'aifêng Fu and his present state, and he compared with pride the splendour of his proposed marriage with the ignominy which attached to his former alliance. His mind scarcely reverted to the midnight scene in the boat. He had written to tell Mr Chu of "the sad event," and had received in reply a piteous letter full of grief, and then, so far as he was concerned, the matter had ended. He was not of an imaginative turn of mind; and so soon as all danger to himself had disappeared, his spirits revived, and his mind recovered its wonted serenity. Le was the only man who could bring evidence against him, and he was fast bound in prison, and was, if report said rightly, likely to exchange his cell for the execution-ground. He therefore prepared the wedding-presents with a light heart, and penned the following epistle to accompany them :—

"With joy and humility I rejoice that your Excellency has deigned to give your consent to the marriage of your beloved one with me. The approach of the time when I may taste of the feathery verdure of the matrimonial peach fills me with delight, and I trust that our union may establish an alliance between our two families which shall stand as firm as the heavenly tripod. I send herewith some mean and paltry presents, which I pray your Excellency to receive."

"Prostrate," wrote the Intendant in reply, "I received your honourable presents; and I look forward with pleasure to the time when the red cords of Destiny[1] shall bind your feet to those of my despicable daughter. I am heartily ashamed to send the accompanying paltry gifts in exchange for your magnificent presents; but I beg you to excuse my deficiencies. On the 15th of next month I shall await the arrival of your jade chariot, and the emblematic geese[2] will be ready prepared in my mean dwelling."

As the wedding-day drew near, Pearl became more and more anxious as to the wisdom of the step she was about to take; and if it had not been for the support she received from Ting, she would even at the eleventh hour have evaded the engagement. Green-jade, in whom the love she had borne towards Wang was turned to bitterest contempt and hate,

[1] Destiny, it is believed, binds the feet of those who are to be united in marriage with red cords.

[2] Geese are the emblems of conjugal fidelity.

could not cordially recommend her former rival to take upon herself again the yoke which had proved so uncongenial, and Peony had no words in which to express her disapproval of the arrangement.

"I would as soon hold out my head under the executioner's knife as marry that man again, if I were you, madam."

"He has probably seen the errors of his ways by this time," said Pearl, "and will, I have no doubt, make a good husband in the future."

"The proverb says, 'The body may be healed, but the mind is incurable,'" replied Peony; "and until I see a leopard change its spots, I will not believe that that mean and cruel man can ever be reformed."

"Well, perhaps it was my fault," said Pearl, "that he was not better at first. Besides, he will no longer have Le to lead him astray. I will cap your proverb with the saying, 'A yielding tongue endures'; and as I intend to be yielding in everything, I have every confidence that Wang will turn out as good as he has been bad."

"One more proverb and I have done," said Peony. "'Ivory does not come from a rat's mouth.' But as you have made up your mind, I will say no more. I will only ask that if Mr Ting will give leave, we should follow a custom, when introducing Mr Wang into your chamber, which is common in my part of the country."

"What is that?" said Pearl.

"We make the bridegroom run the gauntlet between old women armed with switches," said Peony; "and it is such fun to see the way they run."

Ting, on being consulted, readily gave his consent to Peony's proposal, and even hinted that if *she* stood among the old women with a stouter switch than usual, he should make no objection.

"Only confine your custom to Mr Wang, if you please, Miss Peony," he added; "I have no inclination to have my shoulders switched."

On the eventful day Wang arrived dressed in canonicals, and full of that satisfaction which small minds feel at the achievement of social success. He received the congratulations of the subordinate officials with haughty condescension, and conversed affably with Ting before the ceremonies began. He went through his part with perfect composure, which is more than can be said for Pearl and Green-jade, who, if they had not been concealed behind their wedding-veils, would have broken down entirely. At last the vows having been made to Heaven, Earth, and the ancestors of the brides and bridegrooms, and the marriage-feast having been brought to a conclusion, the bridegrooms were conducted to the apartments of their brides. As Wang crossed the hall leading to his bridal chamber, a number of old women, headed by Peony, formed up in double line, and as the unconscious Wang passed between them, each drew from her ample sleeve a stick with which she belaboured the unfortunate bridegroom. It did Peony's heart good to see how the stately swagger with which he entered their ranks became a hasty flight, as the blows rained upon his shoulders. A parting blow which Peony aimed with nervous strength on his luckless head drew a cry of pain

"WANG."

from him, and he rushed headlong into his wife's room, almost tripping over the door-curtain in his haste to reach a place of safety.

Pale and breathless he stood before the veiled figure of his wife, and it was some seconds before he could sufficiently recover his nerves to raise the red veil which concealed Pearl's features. When he did so he started back with horror and amazement. The little presence of mind which remained to him deserted him entirely. He trembled all over, and putting his hand before his eyes, cried, "Take it away, take it away! What fool's trick is this?"

So saying, he turned and ran towards the door, where he encountered Ting.

"Whither away?" said that gentleman. "You run from your wife as though she were the plague. Have you had a quarrel already?"

"Let me go," replied Wang. "Either she is a ghost, or some trick has been played upon me."

"She is no ghost, but your wife Pearl, whom now for the second time you have married. Speak to your husband, lady."

"I am indeed doubly your wife," said Pearl. "And I trust that our second nuptials will be the prelude to a longer and happier wedded existence than was vouchsafed to us by the gods before."

At these words, and fortified by the presence of Ting, Wang regained enough composure to glance furtively at Pearl, the placidity and good temper of whose features bore in upon him the consciousness that he had nothing to fear from her. This conviction gave him courage.

"But how has this all happened?" he said. "Is it possible that you were saved from drowning in the rapid?"

"It is possible," said Ting. "And now let me lead you to your wife's side, and I will then leave her to explain it all."

So saying, he led him to a seat beside his wife, and then retired.

In as few words as were possible, Pearl related how she had been saved, and enlarged with warmth on the kindness she had received from Ting. Not a word of reproach did she utter, and she gave him to understand by her manner that the past was forgotten.

Tortured by a remorse which was awakened by her presence, and fearful lest Ting should take a more judicial view of his conduct than she did, Wang fell on his knees before his wife and implored her forgiveness, vowing at the same time that he would be a true and kind husband to her for the rest of his life. Pearl hastily raised him from the ground, and assured him that, so far as both she and Ting were concerned, what had happened would be as though it had never taken place. Peace was thus restored; and as with advancing night quiet took possession of the courtyards, so harmony reigned in the bridal chambers.

After ten years of most undeservedly placid married life, Wang was stricken down with fever, and in a vision of the night a spirit passed before his face. Trembling and terrified he gazed into the darkness, and though he could see nothing, he was conscious that some form stood before him. He was too frightened to cry out, and after a silence which seemed to him to last for hours, he heard a voice saying—

"According to the original decree of the God of Hades, you should have fifteen more years of life before you; but inasmuch as you have been guilty of the heinous crime of attempting to murder your wife, the thread of your existence is about to be snapped."

With these words the vision vanished, and Wang fell back unconscious. In this condition Pearl found him a few minutes later, and as the morning light broke through the lattice-window his spirit passed into the land of forgetfulness.

"I am indeed doubly your wife."—Page 174.

HOW A CHINESE B.A. WAS WON.

ABOUT two centuries before the time of Abraham, the emperor who then sat upon the throne of China ordained that triennial examinations should be held among the officials of the empire, in order that the "unworthy might be degraded and the meritorious promoted to honour." The plan answered excellently well, we are told, and would probably have thenceforth become a recognised part of the machinery of government, had not evil times fallen upon the country. The peace which reigned so long as the virtuous sovereigns Shun and Yu (B.C. 2255-2197) occupied the throne, disappeared with the death of Yu, and disorder spread like a flood over the empire. In the council-chambers of the succeeding emperors, armed warriors took the place of the learned scholars who had advised their predecessors, and no examination, but such as tried the strength of their right arms and their skill in warlike fence, found favour with these soldiers of fortune for an instant.

Thus, though at intervals the nation returned to its right mind under the guidance of wise and beneficent rulers, the scheme inaugurated by Shun fell into abeyance, and it was not until nearly three thousand years later that Yang-te (A.D.) 605-617 varied the monotony of his otherwise profligate reign by reinstituting a system of examination for office. Unlike everything European, and therefore thoroughly Chinese, the highest degree was instituted first, and the lowest last. Yang-te, like Shun, began by examinations among his courtiers. His successors, arguing that what was good for the courtiers would be good for the people at large, ordained that "search should be made each year in every prefecture and district for elegant scholars and dutiful sons," who should, after satisfying the examiners, be employed in the State.

In this way were called into being the three degrees which exist at the present day—viz., the Siu-ts'ai, or Elegant Scholar; the Keu-jin, otherwise Heaou-leen, or Dutiful Son; and Tsin-sze, or Advanced Scholar, the earlier creation of Yang-te. The same books also upon which it was ordained that the candidates should be examined eleven hundred years ago, are still used for the like purpose. But as with advancing culture the number of competitors have multiplied exceedingly, it has become obviously impossible that offices should be found for all those who are successful; and the contests, especially for the lowest degree of Siu-ts'ai, have ceased to be for anything more than the honour of the degree. Those who succeed in becoming Tsin-sze are, as a general rule, appointed at once to the mandarinate, and a Keu-jin who has influence in high quarters generally gets employment; but the degree of Siu-ts'ai does nothing more than qualify the holder for official life. Unfortunately for the chances of these pass-men, the practice of drawing all officials from the *literati* has fallen into desuetude; and to such an extent has this departure from ancient custom been carried, that nearly one-half of the mandarins of the present day have, it is said, never faced the examiners. Still the competitive examinations form the only officially recognised road to the mandarinate, and this alone is enough to keep the examiners' lists full. But, apart from this consideration, the high value which is attached by tradition to literary culture induces every one in whom glimmers the least intellectual light to tempt fortune in the examination-hall. The first ambition of every self-made man is that a son may be born to him who will reflect glory on his grey hairs by winning a degree. He feels that his acquired wealth is as nothing to him, so long as his household is without the wearer of a buttoned cap to raise it above the families of the people, and to link it with the inhabitants of *yamuns* (*i.e.*, official residences).

Such a one was Le Tai, the great salt merchant, who gave the name of Le-chia Chwang to the village where he lived. He had begun life in a very small way, having been a junior clerk in the office of a farmer of the salt *gabelle*, to whose business he eventually succeeded. By constant perseverance, and by the help of some well-devised ventures, he gradually accumulated so considerable a fortune that, when his employer signified his intention of retiring, he was able to pay him down a good round sum for the goodwill of the business, and to set at rest some official cravings which it was necessary to satisfy before he could obtain the Salt Commissioner's seal to his appointment. Fortune had been kind also to him in his domestic relations. The two sons who grew up before him were a double assurance to him that the sacrifices at his tomb would be duly and regularly offered. He had daughters too, but they satisfied no ambition and dissipated no fear, and he laid, therefore, no great store on their existence. Not that he was an unkind father. On the contrary, he was fond of toying with his little daughters, but his heart was with his sons, Le Taou and Le Ming.

Taou had at an early age developed a taste for the counting-house, and was rapidly becoming as skilled as his father in driving bargains and defrauding the revenue. Ming, on the other hand, had, from his childhood up, displayed a studious bent of mind. When little more than an infant he would stand in the village school with his face to the wall and his hands behind his back, after the recognised fashion, and repeat, without stumbling, the "Three Character Classic" at the top of his voice, heedless of the like shrill utterances of the young Wangs and Changs who, envious of his superior attainments, declaimed in his ears their by no means perfect lessons. From such promising beginnings he made rapid strides in his studies, until, as he now boasts, he could say with Confucius that "at fifteen he bent his mind to learning." Under the guidance of a tutor, whose title to teach consisted only in the fact of his having, after many ineffectual efforts, taken the lowest degree of Siu-ts'ai some twenty years before, he made himself master of the "Five Classics" and "Four Books," and could talk with equal fluency on the eight diagrams of Fuh-he, the doctrine of the "Superior Man," and the excellences of the "Mother of Mencius." His acquaintance with the interpretations put upon these texts by every scholar, from K'ung Ying-ta to Yuen Yuen, was profound; and his knowledge of rites and ceremonies was such as to put to shame his less cultured father and brother. His scrupulous attention to every deferential observance inculcated in the rites of Chow proclaimed him a scholar, but marked him in their minds as a prig. He was not a lively companion, for his studies, instead of making him think or rousing his imagination, had only stored his mind with philosophical platitudes and well-worn truisms. But as the accumulation of a good stock of these was essential to enable him to pass the examination which would make him a possible mandarin, his friends put up with his references to Confucius and the other sages, and allowed themselves to be bored to death with his odes and essays. It was quite a relief to them, however, when, as the examination drew near, he betook himself to a summer-house in the garden, whither he carried his books and "the four precious things" of a scholar's study—viz., pencil, paper, ink, and inkslab. Here he spent his days and a great part of his nights in learning by heart the Nine Classics, laboriously conning the commentaries, and getting up the contents of the rhyming dictionaries. Once or twice he allowed himself to be enticed by his *quondam* schoolfellows, Wang and Chang, who also hoped to face the Literary Chancellor, into a picnic up the river to a Buddhist monastery embosomed in trees among the mountains. On these occasions the friends, as became scholars, lightened their feast by making couplets; and as he who failed in his task had to drink three cups of wine, it not unfrequently happened that Ming was, on the morning after such expeditions, more fit for his bed than his books. When he declared his intention of giving up these merry-makings as interfering with his work, his friends laughed at him, and confided to him their intention of smuggling "sleeve" editions of the classics into the examination-hall, plaited in their queues, and advised him to do the same. But Ming, though inclined at first to yield to the temptation, refused, and went back to his summer-house and his books. From these nothing now withdrew him—not even the artifices of Kin Leen, the pretty waiting-maid of Miss Ling next door, who one day threw over the wall, so as to fall in front of his study window, a stone with a bit of paper tied to it. Ming picked it up, and found the paper to contain a couplet, which it did not require his deep reading to discover was an invitation to him to take the reverse direction of the stone. But he crunched the note in his hand and buried his face in the 'Book of Changes.'

"Ming picked it up, and found the paper to contain a couplet."

But soon the time came when he thought himself ripe for examination for the degree of Siu-ts'ai; so one morning he presented himself at the Le-fang department of the magistrate's *yamun* in the neighbouring city, and demanded of the secretary in charge the conditions under which he could appear at the next ordeal. "First of all," said the secretary, who was not in a good humour that morning, "if you are the son of an actor, or a servant, it is no use your coming, for such people are not allowed to compete at all. But if you are not, you must send us, in writing, your name and age, your place of residence, the names of your father, your mother, your grandfather and grandmother, your great-grandfather and great-grandmother. And further, you must give us a description of your appearance, the colour of your complexion, and whether you have any hair on your face. And now I must attend to other business."

Acting on this hint, Ming made his bow, and as soon as he got home he sat down to supply the information required of him. He had some difficulty in going as far back as his great-grandparents, and when he came to the question of the colour of his complexion he hesitated, and would have liked to describe it as white, but after consulting the glass he saw the truth was too obvious, so he wrote "yellow." Armed with this paper, he returned to the *yamun*, and when it had been examined and pronounced satisfactory, he was allowed to take away a packet of examination paper. Each morning after this he walked into the city and past the *yamun*, in the hope of seeing the official notice fixing the date of the next examination.

At last, one day, as he turned the corner of the principal street, he saw a crowd at the *yamun* gate, standing before a fresh placard. In his excitement he forgot for a moment the Confucian maxim, never to walk quickly, and he had almost broken into a run before the recollection of the words of the sage steadied his pace. As he came up, Wang met him with a face full of excitement: "His Honour has appointed the 5th of next month," said he; "so we have now got ten more days for work, and as I have been rather idle of late I shall go straight home and make up for lost time."

Ming scarcely heard what he said, but pushed into the crowd to read for himself the notification. True enough, it was as Wang had reported. The 5th was to be the day, and full of his tidings Ming went home to give the news to his parents. From that time he was treated with the consideration due to one who is about to take his first great step in life, and, as the excitement prevented his working, he spent most of his time in visiting those of his friends who were to be among his competitors, and talking over with them their respective chances. One thing filled him with alarm. As the day drew near he learned that he was to be one of upwards of two thousand competitors for the degrees.

Daylight on the 5th saw crowds of students on their way to the Kaopêng-tsze, or examination-hall, in the magistrate's *yamun*. As soon as they had all assembled the doors were thrown open at the upper end of the hall, and the magistrate entered and seated himself at a table covered with red cloth, on which were arranged pencils, inkstones, and paper, and at which also sat the secretaries who were to assist in the examination. Presently, amid a deathlike silence, a notice-board was displayed, on which it was announced that the work for the day would consist of an essay on the passage from the Lun-yu: "The Master said, 'Is it not pleasant to learn with a constant perseverance and application?'" another essay on the passage, also from the Lun-yu: "A youth should overflow with love for all men;" and a poem on "Wine," after the manner of the poets of the T'ang dynasty.

Instantly two thousand pencils were seized by as many nervous and eager hands, and the work of the day began. Fortunately for Ming, the commentator's remarks on the first passage were tolerably fresh in his recollection, so that he was able to start off without delay. "Learning," he wrote, "is only the first step towards perfection, and he who desires to become a superior man must strive daily to improve his knowledge and perfect his understanding. But the Master's words have also a wider signification. They are intended to impress upon us that in every concern we undertake we must not only begin, but must also make an end. It is better not to begin a matter than, having begun, to leave it unfinished. But let us further consider this text. It is with the whole body that we pursue after an object, but it is with the heart that we accomplish it. Let us therefore try to keep our hearts pure and our intentions sincere, and we shall then be able to do great things. But how are we to keep our hearts pure?" And then he went on with some very excellent Confucianism to answer his own question, and brought his essay to a conclusion with a eulogy on the supreme wisdom of the text.

Flushed with his first success, he took up his second paper; but his views, or rather those he had imbibed from the commentators Chu He, Ch'ing Hao, and others, were not so clearly defined on the love with which a youth should regard all men, as on the first text. However, he began: "In this passage it is important to bear in mind the distinction the Master would draw between the love of a youth and the love of a full-grown man. A youth brought up within his father's house has no experience of the world, and has not arrived at that knowledge when it is safe for him to hate as a man should hate, or love as a man should love. The Master said that he hated those who spoke evil of others, those who slandered their superiors, and those who were forward and violent, and, at the same time, of contracted understanding. It is fitting, therefore, that men should rightly hate as well as rightly love. But how can a youth who is still unlearned decide for himself whom to love and whom to hate? Therefore the Master says 'he should love all men." Here his memory failed him, and as he was incapable of any original thought, he would have had to lay down his pencil had it not occurred to him that he might drag into his essay a panegyric on the love of children for their parents. The idea was a happy one, and enabled him to complete the required number of lines before poor Wang, who sat near him, had done much more than write down the text.

But the poem he felt to be a more serious matter than either of the essays. Fortunately the subject was one upon which his favourite author Le Tai-pĭh had repeatedly written, and finding that he had still plenty of time before him, he shut his eyes and tried to recall to his recollection the praises which that great wine-loving poet had lavished on the bottle. Gradually his memory summoned up lines and parts of lines and conventional expressions in sufficient quantity to enable him to begin the mosaic, which he was fully aware must make up any poetical effusion on his part. After much "ploughing with the pencil" and long mental struggles, he wrote as follows:—

"When o'er the village shines the evening sun,
And silent stand the tombs of bygone men,
When birds sing evening chant beside the way,
Then sit you down to drink your perfumed wine.
The men of old did quickly pass the flask,
And sharp of wit did improvise their songs,
Then youths were only bidden to the feasts
Who drained their goblets to the latest drop."

With this final effort his work for the day was over, and he returned home with the happy consciousness that he had done well. For the benefit of his anxious friends he had to fight his mental battle o'er again, and he retired to bed to dream of honours lost and won; and just as he imagined himself introduced into the imperial presence as *Chwang-yuen*, or first literate of the year, he was roused by his father, who came to tell him that the morning was breaking, and that it was time to be up and stirring. The sun had scarcely risen on the earth when he found himself once again in the examination-hall surrounded by his fellow-competitors of yesterday. Again the magistrate took his seat at the table, and without further preface it was announced that the work for that day, which would be the last of that examination, would consist of three essays: one on the passage from the Le Ke—"Tsze-shang's mother died, and he did not mourn for her. His father's disciples therefore asked of Tsze-sze, 'In bygone days did not Confucius mourn for his divorced mother?'" Another on the text from the Classic of Filial Piety: "The Master said, 'Formerly the intelligent kings served their fathers with filial piety, and therefore they served heaven with intelligence; they served their mothers with filial piety, and therefore they served earth with discrimination.'" And a third upon the passage from the Sing-le or Mental Philosophy of Chu He: "Water belongs to the female principle of nature, yet it has its root in the male; fire belongs to the male principle, yet it has its root in the female."

By the time the papers were handed in Ming felt that he had written three fairly good essays. On several occasions during the day his attention had been attracted to his next neighbour, an old man, whose trembling hand seemed scarcely able to trace the characters he wished to write. His ideas also evidently flowed slowly, and Ming had several times longed to be able to offer him suggestions. How much they were needed was obvious from the unfinished state of the papers the old scholar handed in at the close of the day, and his dejected mien as he left the hall showed that he was painfully conscious of his shortcomings. But, truth to tell, the feeling that he had done well soon drove the recollection of the veteran out of Ming's mind, and he hurried home to satisfy the eager expectancy of his parents with the tale of his exploits. He knew, however, that his success would have to remain problematical until the publication of the lists in two or three days' time; and he wisely determined to give himself the rest which he felt he needed, and not to attempt to read for the second five-day examination, which he knew he would have to face almost immediately if his name should now appear in the charmed circle of successful competitors.

On the third day he went into the city to see if by chance the lists were published, and found the streets thronged by his associates, who had come on the same fruitless errand as himself. As, after mid-day, there was no hope of his anxieties being set at rest before the morrow, he allowed himself to be tempted by some of his fellow-students to join them in a picnic to a suburban garden, where the pleasure-seekers amused themselves by extemporising couplets and drinking wine among the flowers. Towards evening the fun grew fast and furious, and Ming found it necessary at last to retreat to a secluded summer-house to sleep off the effects of his potations before returning home. His debauch, however, did not prevent his being in the city early the next morning, as it had been reported among his *convives* of the previous evening that the lists would be out soon after daybreak. On entering the gates he was met by a candidate, by whose excited appearance Ming saw at once that his fate was sealed one way or the other. "The lists are out," said his friend, "and my name is in the circle." "I congratulate you," answered Ming, "and may you rise to office and reap emoluments! But where does my name appear?" "I had not time to look," said his friend as he hurried on. With all possible speed Ming made his way to the magistrate's *yamun*, outside the walls of which he saw an excited crowd gathered round a long strip of paper, covered for the most part with names written perpendicularly, but having at one end a circle composed of the centrifugally written names of those who had passed best. When fairly within sight of the paper which was to resolve his doubts, Ming suddenly felt an inclination to slacken his pace and to look in at the shop-windows. At last, however, he made his way into the crowd, and had just discovered his name in the circle when an acquaintance cried out, "Ah! Le Laou-ye,[1] I congratulate you. My name is only two from yours. But I am afraid our poor friend Wang is left out in the cold." "I am sorry for that," replied Ming, "but let me congratulate you on your success. Have you heard when the second examination is to be held?" "In two days' time. May you become a *chwang-yuen!* Good-bye." "And may you have a seat at the Feast of the Blowing of the Deer!"[2] replied Ming, as he hurried off homewards to announce his good fortune.

At the news of his son's success the old salt mer-

[1] A complimentary title equivalent to "your worship."

[2] A feast given to the graduates at the provincial examinations.

chant's joy knew no bounds, and he instantly issued invitations for a feast on the next afternoon in commemoration of the event. In the meantime the house was besieged by friends—more especially poor ones—who came to congratulate Ming, and who exhausted every good wish it was possible to devise for his future happiness and advancement. In the estimation of his mother and sisters his success had already raised him on a pinnacle of fame; and, after their first burst of joy was over, his mother reminded him that a go-between had been to her several times to propose a marriage for him with Miss Yang, the daughter of an ex-Prefect living in the neighbourhood; "and now that you are on the fair road to office," added she, "do let me authorise her to open negotiations." "Let us wait until I have made a name for myself by taking my degree," answered her son, "and then I will obey your wishes in that as in all other respects."

In the pleasurable enjoyment of being made much of, the two days' interval passed quickly to Ming, and the morning of the third day found him seated again in the magistrate's hall, surrounded by all his former competitors, with the exception of a few whose names had figured so near the tail of the long straight list that they had recognised the hopelessness of competing any more. The same old man who had excited his compassion at the first examination was there, however, looking excited and nervous. Ming was now the more sorry for him, as he had recognised his name almost last upon the list; but the entrance of the magistrate presently drove all thoughts but those on the subjects before him out of his head.

This examination, it was announced, was, as usual, to last five days. The course on each of the first four days was to consist of an essay on a text taken from the 'Four Books,' as well as of a poem. On the third day an ode on a given subject was to be optional, and on the fourth day an opportunity was promised to aspiring candidates of writing additional poems. On the fifth day the work was to consist only of half an essay on a theme from the 'Four Books.'

At this examination Ming worked with varying success. His profound knowledge of the classics and the writings of the commentators stood him in good stead, and his constant study of the T'ang dynasty poets was amply rewarded by the way in which they honoured his drafts on them to meet his poverty of ideas. The ode on the third day, which was "On the Pleasure men take in talking of the Signs of the Seasons," exercised his imagination to the utmost. Thrice he put pencil to paper, and as often he tore to shreds his lines. The fourth time he wrote as follows, and, as the hour of closing was drawing near, he handed the result in with his other compositions:—

> "When the belated guest his host reseeks,
> And cloudless skies proclaim the close of day,
> 'Tis sweet to talk of treacherous weather past,
> And watch the dying sun's effulgent ray."

Ming was no poet, but even he felt that his lines lacked freshness of ideas and vigour of diction. He was conscious, however, of having made one or two happy turns in the rhymes, which, truth to tell, were borrowed from some old published examination papers;

but, knowing the somewhat pedantic literary taste of the magistrate, he founded some hopes upon them. And he was right. After a few days of suspense his name appeared on the walls of the *yamun*, high up in the list of successful candidates. Again the rejoicings at Le-chia Chwang were repeated, and again congratulations poured in upon him from all sides. Even the ex-Prefect, upon whose daughter Mrs Le was keeping her eye, deemed the occasion of sufficient importance to warrant a note, which he sent, accompanied with a red-lacquer tray full of dainty dishes and luscious sweets, some of which Mrs Le shrewdly suspected had been prepared by the delicate fingers of Miss Yang. This was the most gratifying recognition that Ming had as yet received, and he took the letter from the servant reverentially in both hands. Eagerly he tore open the envelope, and read as follows:—

"In ancient times men's merits were judged by the speed with which they chased a deer, the fleetest of foot winning the prize. But now the way to fame is bridged by learning, and for many years it has been my fate to speed and bid farewell to old friends like yourself, who fly on the wings of success to the capital. Of all the batches of brilliant scholars who have ever passed at these examinations, I hear that that to which you have lent your countenance, and which has now entered the epidendrum city[1] of the learned, is the most conspicuous. Humbly I offer you the paltry things which with this letter I lay at your feet, and respectfully long for the sound of the gold fastening of your response."

[1] *I.e.*, the joyous company.

Scarcely had Ming replied to this flattering epistle when a messenger arrived with an invitation from the magistrate to dinner on the following day. As it was in accordance with immemorial usage that the successful candidates should be entertained by the magistrate, this summons was no surprise to so keen a student of rites and ceremonies as Ming; and on the next afternoon he went in a sedan-chair to the *yamun*, fully prepared for the company he found assembled there. But he was much flattered by the way in which the magistrate received him. "Your honourable essays are genuine pearls of literature," said his host, "and you are possessed of a supply of classical knowledge which cannot but gain you admittance to the Dragon (*i.e.*, imperial) presence." "Your honour overrates the mean pencil-scratchings of this dullard, and allows the reflection of your lofty genius to brighten the inelegancies of his wretched compositions," replied Ming. This speech he had carefully prepared as he came along in his chair, on the chance of his having to reply to a complimentary greeting. His fellow-students, however, being unaware of his forethought, sang aloud their praises of his readiness as they sat down to the feast. Before starting, Mrs Le had strictly enjoined Ming to bring back an account of the good things he was to partake of, and in obedience to her orders he stored his memory with the following list of dishes:—

Bêche de mer; stewed duck, served with force-meat; birds'-nest soup; hashed pigeon, with ham; stewed crabs; fried black fish; stewed mutton, with bamboo shoots; fowl and ham; turtle-soup; hashed dog; stewed black cat; fried rat; macaroni-soup; salt fish; salted eggs; minced pork; basins of rice; and an infinite variety of fruits and sweets.

Before beginning, the magistrate poured out a libation, and without more ado the guests set to work at the good things before them. The wine circulated freely, and lent material aid to the magistrate in his endeavours to set every one at his ease. To Ming the magistrate showed marked attention, and with his own chopsticks carried a fine slug from the dish to the lips of the favoured guest, a compliment which made quite a stir among the other scholars. Not far from Ming, but apart from every one, sat the old student whom he had noticed in the examination-hall, but whose want of success scarcely entitled him to a seat at the feast. Some such remark Ming made to the magistrate, who explained that each year a certain number of degrees were given away to plucked old students, and that he was going to recommend his guest for one on this occasion. After dinner Ming made a point of congratulating the old man, who in quavering accents made a pedantically complimentary reply, every word of which was taken from the 'Four Books.' Wang, Ming noticed, was not among the invited, and the magistrate told him that though there were clever thoughts and much sound reasoning in his essays, yet it was too plain that his knowledge of the texts of the classics and the views of the commentators were not sufficiently thorough to pass him, and that therefore he had been obliged to advise him to come up again next time.

From private sources Ming heard that Wang was sorely disappointed at his want of success, so the next morning he wrote him the following note of condolence: "The decayed willows on the Sin-ting Pass sent forth a sweet savour, and rotten T'ung trees delighted Tsai Yung[1] with their melody. If a jewel be encased in a hidden casket, it is not every sword which can cleave it so as to display the jewels[2] found by Pien Ho on the King Mountain, or the pearls snatched by the Earl Suy from the serpent's head. Who can explain the lofty talents enjoyed by some, or account for the meaner abilities bestowed on others? We are as we are made, and there is no helping ourselves." To this kindly epistle Wang sent reply:—

"Well may I adopt the lines of Chang Shu as my chant—

'A thousand miles o'er sea and fields
I have followed at your horse's heels;
I have travelled over hill and dale,
And now have missed the dragon's scale.'[3]

Gratefully I acknowledge your sympathetic words, in which I recognise the lofty nature which has en-

[1] A celebrated scholar and musician of the second century. It is recorded of him that while seated at the fireside of a friend in the State of Wu, his attention was attracted to the sounds emitted from a log of a T'ung tree which was burning on the hearth, and declaring that its tone gave promise of rare excellence, he converted it into a lute.

[2] A block of jade which, being believed to be spurious, was rejected by two emperors in succession, the last of whom condemned Pien Ho (eighth century B.C.) to lose his left foot as an impostor. The next emperor, however, perceiving the genuineness of the stone, graciously accepted it, and offered Pien Ho a title of nobility, which he declined.

[3] *I.e.*, "And now have missed taking my degree." The idea, a poetical one, being that a successful scholar resembles a soaring dragon.

abled you to overcome all the difficulties in your path. Though incapable through grief to write, I fear to return you a verbal message. As night approaches my sorrow almost seems to weigh me down, and I wrap myself in a cattle cloak, after the manner of Wang Chang,[1] and weep bitter tears. What else is left for me to do?"

Ming knew that he would now have a respite of two or three months before the time came for him to be examined by the Prefect, as a preliminary to his going up for his final examinations before the Literary Chancellor. He retired therefore again to his summer-house, and devoted himself to a renewed study of the books which had already served him so well. As the day drew near, his father wrote to an old friend at the prefectural city, asking him to receive his son for the examination, and, in response to a cordial invitation which was returned, Ming mounted his mule one morning at daybreak, and started off on his momentous journey. Late in the evening he reached the hospitable door of his father's friend, and woke the next morning, after a sound sleep, refreshed and ready for the work before him. After eating a hasty breakfast, he hurried off to the *yamun* of the Literary Chancellor, and arrived only just in time, for he had scarcely got into the hall when a gun was fired as a signal for the fast closing of the doors. The arrangements he found to be in all respects similar to those at the magistrate's *yamun*, and the subjects for examination were taken from the

[1] A well-known character, who, after enduring great poverty, afterwards became a metropolitan magistrate.

same books, the only difference being that the Prefect's more liberal mind was reflected in the texts he had chosen for the essays. With each of his five days' work Ming was fairly satisfied, and when the examination was over he waited with some acquired confidence for the publication of the result. The appearance of his name, however, in the first flight of successful competitors was none the less a delight to him, and he sent off an express messenger to Le-chia Chwang to proclaim his success to his parents. "Your stupid son," he added, "is but waiting to obey the invitation sent him by his Excellency the Prefect to dinner to-morrow before hastening to your honourable dwelling to throw himself at your feet." The dinner at the Prefect's was very much a repetition of that given by the magistrate, except that there was a marked weeding out in point of numbers. The reputation which Ming had brought with him for scholarship, and which he had just maintained, ensured him friendly notice at the hand of the Prefect, who, however, did not seem much to relish his stilted style of conversation and his Confucius-or-nothing train of thought. Before the students parted their host announced that, as usual, he should send the seat numbers and not the names of the successful competitors to the Literary Chancellor, who would hold the final examinations on that day month in that city.

The next day Ming went home, and was met at the entrance of the village by a number of his associates, who greeted him with cries of congratulation. The welcome he received from his immediate family was especially joyous, and for days a succession of visitors poured in upon him to offer their felicitations on his marked and sustained success. Under such agreeable circumstances he took little heed of time, and almost before Ming was aware he was reminded that it was time to betake himself again to the prefectural city. The merchant who had been his host on the previous occasion was glad enough once more to open his doors to a scholar who was already winning for himself eminence; and though he cared little for his companionship, preferring lively and suggestive conversation to dull platitudes and measured periods, he paid him marked deference, as one to whom the door of office, the highest object of ambition, would soon be opened.

The ordeal Ming was now called upon to face was more terrible to him than any of the other examinations had been. Up to this time he had presented himself only before the local officials, men whom he had constantly seen, and with whom he was in a sense familiar. Besides, hitherto the contests had been but preliminary, whereas the examinations in which he had now to compete were either to make or to mar him, at all events temporarily; and the examiner was surrounded with all the dignity and awe of an unknown great personage. It was with no slight trepidation, therefore, that he took his seat again on stool No. 33, by which number he was known for the time being. As soon as the gun was fired and the door shut, the Chancellor entered. As he approached the table, all rose, and every eye was turned towards the man in whose hands their fate rested. He was of medium height, and a plump figure, with a round good-natured face, a pair of small twinkling eyes, and a long scanty moustache. After bowing politely to the students, he seated himself at the table and straightway proclaimed on the notice-board that on this occasion he should require from them two essays on the texts from the 'Four Books': "The Master said, 'It is by the odes that the mind is aroused; it is by the rules of propriety that the character is established; and it is from music that the finish is received.'" And, "When a ruler sympathises in his people's joys, they take pleasure in his rejoicings; and when he shares their sorrows, they sympathise with his griefs." And a poem on the "Pleasure of hearing the notes of a distant lute amid the sound of drippings from the roof on a wet day."

Ming was too nervous to collect his thoughts and set his memory at work at once, and it was some time before he put pencil to paper. But when he did, he made fair progress, and at the end of the day he had the satisfaction of knowing that if his essays contained no new or striking thoughts, they were at all events thoroughly orthodox, and that the sentences were framed in accordance with the rules laid down by some of the best-known essayists. He was rather disappointed, therefore, to find, when the list of eighty optimes came out, that "Thirty-three" was barely within the first forty. This was the first check of any kind which he had met with, and it alarmed him; for he gathered from it that the Commissioner did not take the same favourable view of his literary matter and manner as the magistrate and prefect had done. It was with a sobered countenance, therefore, that he took his seat again for the second trial. This time several themes were given out from the 'Four Books,' upon which the students were expected to compose half essays. To these Ming devoted his best energies, and was rewarded by finding his number published two days later in the circle of successful competitors.

Having recovered some confidence from this result, Ming took his seat in the hall, on the morning after the publication of the lists, with some assurance. The comparatively small number of competitors, which had been reduced to eighty, or just double the number of degrees competed for, by the Chancellor, gave a silent and business-like air to the assembly. On this occasion the candidates wrote an essay on a text from the 'Four Books,' one on a text from the 'Five Classics,' and a poem. At the close of the day's work the Commissioner announced that after examining the papers he should, as was customary, write to the Prefect for the names of the best men, whom at present he only knew by their numbers, and should at once publish them. "And I have arranged," he added, "that the first competitors from the other districts shall meet you here in ten days' time finally to compete for the degrees." The next few days were spent by Ming in a fever of suspense, which the complimentary speeches of his merchant host were quite ineffectual to allay. To fail now, he felt, would be a terrible blow both to his fortunes and to his pride. What would all his friends say? and what would, above all, the ex-prefect Yang say? However, fortune was kinder to him than his forebodings, and once again he saw with triumph his name among the number of the successful. On this occasion his pleasure was all the greater, since he felt that now he was practically sure of his degree. The final examination spoken of by the Commissioner would, he knew, consist only of a test of his knowledge of the text of the sixteen "Sacred Edicts" of the Emperor K'ang-he, and of "the Amplification" of the same by his son and successor, Yung-Ching. On this point he felt that he could trust his memory to carry him through, for had he not in his study at Le-chia Chwang repeated them over and over again by heart without missing a character? However, to make assurance doubly sure, he devoted some hours of each of the succeeding days to conning them over. On the appointed morning at daybreak he made his way to the Chancellor's hall, where he found assembled his fellow pass-men, together with the picked competitors from the other four districts of the prefecture. There was a semi-holiday air about them all, as though they looked on this trial more as a formality than anything else. The Commissioner, too, entered the hall with a lighter step, and his voice had a cheery tone in it as he ordered the announcement to be made that the morning's work would consist of writing out from memory the seventh edict of the Beneficent Emperor K'ang-he, beginning "Chu e twan," "Flee strange doctrines," with the "Amplification" of the same by his august and intelligent son Yung-Ching.

Fortunately for Ming, this particular edict had been frequently in evidence lately at Le-chia Chwang with reference to the foreign missionary question, which was beginning to disturb that otherwise quiet district. The passage in the "Amplification," *Yew ju se-yang keao tsung T'een chu, yih shuh puh king*—"As to the religion of the Western foreigner which exalts the Lord of Heaven, it is also contrary to our sacred books," &c.—had been constantly quoted in opposition to the proselytising zeal of the missionaries, and the context had been carefully studied by village Confucianists. His task was therefore a comparatively light one, and when he put down his pencil, he felt assured that he had not missed one of the six hundred and forty characters composing the extract. Shortly after noon he walked into his host's family hall, and with so jaunty a step that it needed no words of his to assure his entertainer that he was speaking to a Siu-ts'ai almost *in esse.* It now only remained for him to await the public notification of the final result of the series of examinations which he had gone through during the last two months. On the third day this was published, and the local world was made acquainted with the fact that Le Ming, together with thirty-nine others from the same district, had obtained the degree of Siu-ts'ai. So soon as Ming had despatched a letter with the news to his father, and received the congratulations of his merchant host, he hurried off to one of the first tailors in the city to order the canonicals belonging to his newly acquired honour.

The next day, as in duty bound, the newly made Siu-ts'ais went at the recognised hour to pay their respects to the Chancellor, who received them graciously, and entertained them on tea and sweets, while a band in the courtyard enlivened the company with inspiriting music. Ming was not musical, but even he could not help recognising that well-known and deservedly popular air, "The Autumn Tints stretch across the Sky," and when the musicians struck up the first bars—

he could not resist humming to himself the picturesque refrain—

> "Yao loh ch'iu t'ung,
> Ngai nan chih hwei tsui,
> Yuen k'e tsan t'ung,
> Hao chang shuy k'e kung chwang t'un."

There was one more prescribed ceremony to be gone through before he could return home. On the afternoon following the visit to the Chancellor's, the same gay company went to worship at the temple of Confucius, where, after having prostrated themselves before the image of the Sage, they partook of a feast spread in the courtyard at the expense of the city. Towards evening the scene became one of revelry, and the amount of wine consumed as forfeits in the game of Mora sent many of the guests to bed with "very red cheeks," to "get up very white in the morning." When Ming reached his host's, he found his canonicals had arrived from the tailor's, and, tired though he was, he could not resist the pleasure of trying them on. Early dawn saw him again before the looking-glass, and after a hasty breakfast, he set off for Le-chia Chwang amid the congratulations and good wishes of the worthy merchant and his family. In the evening he reached his home, and when he walked into the family hall, bearing on his person the insignia of his success, his father fairly wept with delight. Nor were the other members of the family less demonstrative as with one consent they offered their congratulations, and expressed their admiration of the becoming and dignified dress which it was now his right to wear. After his mother had carefully examined his silver-buttoned cap, surmounted by a silver bird, his robe of blue silk bordered with black, and his girdle with silver pendants, she whispered in his ear, "And now may I speak to the go-between?"

"Yes, now," replied her son.